# The Secret Chamber Of The Paris Opera

A Novel

Hamon de Quillan

Global East-West. London

# Contents

# Also by the Author

Hamon de Quillan already has four novels to his name (this is his fifth), a collection of short stories and a biographical essay on Faulkner.

## Novels:

Le cercle restreint (The Inner Circle);
Le dernier train pour Paris (The Last Train to Paris);
Le Protocole Méridien (The Meridian Protocol);
La Courtière de l'ombre (The Shadow Broker).

## Short stories:

Récits parisiens: La fille aux cheveux roux suivi par le mystère de l'homme rouge (Parisian Stories: The Girl With the Red Hair And The Mystery of The Red Man).

## Biographical essay:

William Faulkner: Une vie en littérature (William Faulkner: A Life in Literature).

# 1
# The Unexpected Discovery

Footsteps echoed in the darkness, pounding the dusty floor of the Paris Opera House. Gabriel moved cautiously, as if afraid to break the thousand-year silence that inhabited these forgotten places. He had been called in hastily to examine an unusual discovery, lost beneath the centuries-old foundations of the illustrious building. The air was heavy with mystery, charged with a strange atmosphere that enveloped every corner in a spellbinding aura. As he approached an ancient wall, Gabriel felt his heart race. A barely visible crack betrayed the existence of a hidden door.

Carefully, he pushed the ancient door open, revealing a passageway that led into the unknown. As he crossed the dark threshold, his senses were assaulted by an indescribable force, as if the stones themselves were whispering ancient secrets. The flickering torch he held aloft illuminated a huge chamber whose walls were marked with mysterious symbols, carved into the stone by hands long gone. Detailed plans littered the floor, forming a complex puzzle that Gabriel was destined to piece together. The distant echo of ancient voices seemed to ring out in the space, as if whispering the answers to questions he had not yet asked.

The excitement of this extraordinary discovery filled his mind with grand conjectures and hypotheses. At the same time, his soul vibrated in unison with the forgotten builders. At that moment, in an indescribable ballet between shadow and light, he felt bound to this place by an irresistible force. This ancestral connection breathed new passion into his quest for truth. However, as the mystery captured his mind, a threat lurking in the shadows of history began to stir, ready to do anything to preserve the secret buried in the bowels of time.

Night fell like a dark veil over the cobblestones of the sleeping city, enveloping the Paris Opera House in a cloak of mystery. The stars twinkled discreetly, edging the sky with their silvery glow, while the moon, like a celestial sentinel, watched silently. In the hushed darkness, Gabriel stood before the imposing facade of the theatre, feeling a strange sense of irresistible calling coming from the bowels of the earth. An indistinct, almost imperceptible whisper echoed within him, like an invocation from a bygone era.

As he approached the closed doors of the Opera House, he felt an electric tension run through his body, vibrating like a string stretched to its limit. A wave of icy shivers ran through his skin, but instead of backing away, he pushed his fears aside and firmly pressed the handle, opening the way to the unknown. Entering the majestic interior of the building, he was seized by a ghostly vision.

Shadows danced among the columns, sporadically illuminated by the rare glimmers of light filtering through the stained-glass windows. The whispers of history seemed to emanate from the ancient walls, murmuring ancient secrets lost in the mists of time. Walking through the deserted corridors, guided by a force he could not define, Gabriel found his way to a spiral staircase leading down into the depths of the centuries-old building.

A cold breeze brushed his face, adding a touch of mystery to this unexpected descent. At the bottom, he found himself facing a massive door, adorned with mysterious symbols carved into the stone, witnesses to a forgotten era. He did not hesitate, pushing the heavy door open with determination. What greeted him left him speechless.

A secret chamber opened up before him, its walls lined with yellowed parchments, dusty old books, and forgotten relics. In the centre, enthroned like a hidden treasure, lay a table covered with enigmatic patterns, meticulously traced, seeming to whisper forgotten legends.

As he slowly approached, Gabriel felt an incredible sensation, as if time itself had been suspended in this lost chamber. He decided to explore these enigmatic artefacts, aware that each clue could bring him closer to the truth. His fingers brushed the engraved symbols, trying to decipher the forgotten language of that distant era. Suddenly, a fleeting flash illuminated a portion of the ancient writings, revealing an unexpected meaning. Plans intertwined with symbols, forming a complex web of engineering he knew nothing about.

The revelation struck him like a bolt of lightning, awakening a torrent of mixed emotions: fascination, unease, but above all a tremendous thirst for knowledge, propelling him ever further into this quest steeped in mystery. Night fell over the sleeping city, muffling the sounds of the world beneath its cloak of darkness.

In this silent immensity, Gabriel Moreau felt the call of the secret room, coexisting with the echoes of a distant past. His footsteps echoed in the deserted corridors of the Opera House. At the same time, his flashlight swept across the shadows, revealing a macabre ballet of familiar yet unknown shapes.

The walls seemed to whisper ancient secrets, buried memories, like fragments of a forgotten story. And yet, every stone, every crack, every engraved symbol carried within it the promise of an imminent revelation. Suddenly, a cold shiver ran down Gabriel's spine. An invisible presence floated in the thick air, surrounding him with an oppressive aura. Was this the first warning from dark forces determined to dissuade any curious individuals from continuing this obsessive quest?

The tension mounted, pulsing, as Gabriel felt all his senses on alert. The engraved symbols gradually took shape and meaning, like disjointed notes on a musical score waiting to be deciphered, revealing unexpected harmonies.

At the same moment, in another era, Aurélien and Éléonore Desmoulins were also walking the winding path of destiny, secretly joining a circle of free thinkers. Their footsteps echoed in the narrow alleys of Paris, where a breath of rebellion and revolution was stirring. They did not yet know that their story would echo that of Gabriel, intertwining the threads of time to better embrace destinies that mirrored each other and passions that intertwined.

Standing in front of the secret room, Gabriel felt the weight of his family heritage, that indescribable connection that bound him to this mysterious universe. The darkness itself seemed to whisper unspeakable truths, revelations hidden in the depths of centuries. His heart beat to the syncopated rhythm of an imminent discovery, while shadows moved, dancing between reality and illusion. Driven by this irresistible force, he plunged into the depths of the unknown, ready to face the abyss of forbidden knowledge, to defy the darkness and reach the light.

Gabriel's discovery was an enigmatic symphony, blending the darkness of the past with the flashes of light of the present. The plans found in the secret chamber seemed to be the scores of a forgotten opera, revealing ancient mysteries orchestrated by elusive forces. Each symbol engraved on the walls seemed to strike a discordant note in Gabriel's mind, plunging him deeper into an impressive ballet of buried truths. As the shadows of history danced around him, the legends of the past seemed to echo his own discoveries.

Aurélien and Éléonore Desmoulins, embodiments of a tumultuous era, gradually came to life before his astonished eyes. Their stories woven into the fabric of time seemed to echo current events, connecting Gabriel to a legacy he never thought possible. In this dance between darkness and light, Gabriel felt the suffocating embrace of ancient secrets that seemed to weigh heavily on his shoulders.

The centuries-old walls of the room seemed ready to whisper their revelations. However, they still held their breath, prolonging the breathless suspense that tormented Gabriel. Images and memories of the circle of free thinkers haunted Gabriel's thoughts, evoking tales of bravery and perseverance in the face of adversity. He realised that these reminiscences revealed a deeply buried message, like the vibrant themes of a long-forgotten symphony, seeking to captivate an attentive audience.

As the dim light of the lamp flickered in the room, Gabriel let himself be carried away by the grandiose composition unfolding before his eyes. Each discovery was a new measure, each clue a new note, creating a haunting melody that aroused both wonder and unease. Through the veils of time, Gabriel set out to decipher the hidden patterns behind each composition. His mind soared in a dizzying symphony, where the confrontations of the past seemed to clash with the aspirations of the present in a complex and captivating choreography.

It was in this fragile balance between shadow and light that the very essence of his investigation took shape, like the subtle variations of a musical score calling to be interpreted to reveal its ultimate meaning. In the twists and turns of history, some legends resonate like echoes from the past, whispering buried truths and unspeakable mysteries.

It is in these solemn moments that Gabriel Moreau perceives the fleeting brilliance of these legends intertwining with the fabric of his existence. The vibrations of the Paris Opera, silent witnesses to centuries gone by, seem to guide his steps toward an underground world, a hidden chamber whose walls whisper forgotten tales. As he ventures further and further into this fascinating labyrinth, Gabriel feels the growing grip of legend, like a symphony of shadows and light coming to life before his eyes.

Centuries-old frescoes adorn the walls, revealing enigmatic scenes and mysterious arcana, bathed in ancestral darkness. Every line, every symbol, seems to tell an ancient story, awakening in him a sense of fascination mixed with reverential awe. As his steps lead him further into this forgotten world, Gabriel feels transported into a timeless dance, where destinies cross and intertwine, connecting his present to a past that is by turns majestic and dark.

The echoes of ancient legends seem to resonate within him, awakening his curiosity as much as his unease, for behind the veils of mystery lie truths whose revelation could upset the fragile balance of his existence. Like an archaeologist of lost centuries, Gabriel immerses himself in the stories engraved in stone, words, and artistic representations, seeking to understand the many facets of this echoing legend.

Through his research, he realises that the key to these ancient enigmas may lie in an unsuspected harmony between the past and the present, between the history of the Desmoulins family and his own discoveries. Each echo brought back from the past resonates like a missing piece of the puzzle, opening the way to a deeper understanding of this centuries-old legacy. Immersed in this myriad of echoing legends, Gabriel feels a compelling need to pierce the veil of secrecy, decipher the mysterious messages, and give a voice to the forgotten figures of history. Yet, he senses that the road to truth will be fraught with pitfalls, and that the echoes of the past will demand a heavy price to reveal their ancient secrets.


Once upon a time, there was a secret chamber shrouded in mystery, hidden beneath the prestigious Paris Opera House. The walls of this ancient lair echoed with a haunting symphony, engraved in every stone and every corner of space and time. It was there, in this forgotten fortress, that the boundary between eras blurred, giving way to a singular encounter.

Gabriel, immersed in a ballet of shadows and light, was seized by an indescribable fascination. The plans and symbols engraved on the walls seemed to whisper ancient secrets, awakening an indomitable curiosity within him. Like an archaeologist of time, he deciphered the buried remains, unravelling the mysteries of the past that transcended the boundaries of the Opera House.

Meanwhile, like a master painting coming to life, the past (1865) unfolded with disturbing intensity. Aurélien and Éléonore Desmoulins, heirs to an enchanted lineage, crossed the threshold of a circle of free thinkers. Their rebellious aspirations echoed through the ages, intertwining their destinies with Gabriel's in a cosmic dance where the shards of fate mingled. In this room marked by eternity, a first insidious threat emerged, weaving a veil of intimidation worthy of Greek tragedies.

The invisible guardians of history seemed to watch over this precious legacy, exacerbating the daring challenge that was materialising for Gabriel, now a fervent actor in a dark play whose role he did not yet know. Thus, in this temporal waltz, the intoxicating scents of the past tickled the historian's senses, revealing buried secrets and inviting his intrepid mind to dive into the heart of this mystical ocean.

The hidden room beneath history opened its doors wide, letting in a bewitching aura that captured wandering souls through time and heralded the beginning of an enigmatic quest to the ends of the known universe. The Paris Opera, a majestic theatre steeped in history, held many unsuspected mysteries within its walls.

Gabriel stood at the threshold of this secret room, the clues and symbols engraved on the walls illuminating him in the darkness of the past. The plans revealed extraordinary ingenuity, bearing witness to a bygone era when architects competed to hide their creations forever. Studying every detail with passion, Gabriel felt the call of this place, which screamed silently through time.

At the same time, in 1865, the young Aurélien Desmoulins was taking his first steps in a circle of free thinkers. Through the yellowed pages of a diary, the journey of this courageous and rebellious character began to take shape. Accompanied by his sister Éléonore, they embarked on a quest for knowledge and freedom, defying the taboos of the time with disconcerting audacity. Their destinies now seemed linked across generations, weaving an invisible bond between the past and the present. However, this discovery also caused Gabriel concern.

A vague threat hung in the air, creating a feeling of subtle intimidation. It was as if the ancient walls held ancient whispers, revealing the past torments of lost souls. Each of the characters seemed to carry the burden of these forgotten echoes, like an invisible weight dictating the contours of their destiny. Thus, in a whirlwind of time, destinies intertwined, revealing the complexity of human existence.

The shadows of the past seemed to stretch to the far reaches of the present, connecting beings across the centuries. In this eternal dance, where past and present came together in a spellbinding waltz, Gabriel sensed that this quest would take him far beyond the simple boundaries of time, revealing buried truths that no one could predict. Thus, at the heart of this unexpected discovery, the fate of each individual was being played out, drawing lost souls through time in a timeless symphony where past and present became one, ruled by mysterious forces and buried secrets.

The thrilling shivers of excitement crept into Gabriel's veins like a sweet poison, stimulating his mind, hungry for truth. In the timeless vastness of the secret chamber, he carefully observed each engraved symbol, each carefully drawn plan, sensing that these vestiges of the past whispered unfathomable secrets, ready to unravel the mystery that enveloped his passionate soul. The oscillations of time seemed to merge as the echoes of the past resonated in harmony with the present.

The intertwined destinies of Aurélien and Éléonore, like distant stars in the firmament of history, seemed to converge toward a shared fate. Their membership in this clandestine circle of free thinkers, marked by courage and idealism, resonated with Gabriel's ardent quest to pierce the shadows of the past.

Yet, this transcendent alliance between eras was veiled by the insidious threat that hung like a fleeting mist over Gabriel's wanderings. The disturbing whispers of the invisible guardians of ancestral knowledge seemed to oscillate between ardent benevolence and icy dread, permeating the atmosphere of the room with their elusive presence. Every sign, every clue, pulsed with an ancestral energy, defying the continuum of time to reveal itself to those whose minds thirsted for truth.

At the heart of this enigmatic juxtaposition, Gabriel felt a deep vibration, that of the legacy left by his distant ancestors, a legacy steeped in interrupted narratives and unfinished passions. These bold reminiscences, emerging from the forgotten layers of history, exuded a captivating scent of bravery and hope, urging Gabriel to continue his quest with renewed resolve. As twilight enveloped the city in amber hues, Gabriel remained absorbed in the evocative dreams shaped by the depths of the past. The unalterable essence of the first stirrings of an ancient mystery infused his thoughts with an enlightened fervour, giving him the strength to challenge the veils of shadow and reveal the light buried beneath the embrace of time.

The first rays of dawn filtered into the secret room, illuminating the symbols engraved on the centuries-old walls. Gabriel Moreau stood perplexed before the mysterious clues that were gradually being revealed. As his fingers brushed against the inscriptions, he felt a sharp chill run down his spine, as if the stones held ancient secrets ready to be revealed. The im-

palpable dancing dust whispers forgotten stories, destinies intertwined in this forgotten enclave of time. The underground atmosphere
awakens in him a boundless curiosity. It gives
rise to a vibrant intensity, similar to that of great
novelists lost in the heart of their own intrigue.

Meanwhile, in the intertwined narrative of
destiny, the past (1865) is revived with the
meeting of Aurélien and Éléonore Desmoulins,
whirling in circles of avant-garde thought. Their
aspirations and their fiery hopes for a better
world give off a scent of rebellion and daring
idealism that transcends time. An ethereal glow
seems to unite these two distinct timelines,
weaving invisible bonds between generations.

The whispers of the past resonate in harmony with Gabriel's awakening discoveries, as if
every step he takes in this forgotten sanctuary
creates echoes through the centuries. As the
claustrophobia of the underground passages
fades away, a palpable tension emanates from
this timeless encounter between two worlds. A
subtle rumbling of ancient threats disturbs the
calm air, heralding the shadow lurking in the
twists and turns of history. It is in this atmosphere steeped in mystery that the premises of
a timeless adventure take shape, where coinci-
dences light the way to unexpected revelations.

The yellowed pages of the ancient grimoire
exuded a scent of mystery and secrets buried

for centuries. It was there, in that forgotten room beneath the bowels of the Paris Opera, that Gabriel Moreau faced an enigmatic collection of parchments and cryptic codes. The shadows of history seemed to guide him toward revelations hidden in the depths of the night. As his fingers traced the engraved symbols, a sense of urgency crept over him, as if the ancient walls were whispering a silent warning. In a mental whirlwind, the faces of Aurélien and Éléonore Desmoulins, frozen in an antique photograph, materialised before his eyes, timeless witnesses to a past whose echoes seemed to reverberate to him. The surrounding darkness seemed to carry the whispers of the free thinkers of yesteryear.

In contrast, indistinct shapes seemed to come to life in the sepulchral chamber's gloomy glow. The Guardiani Invisibili, the legendary invisible guardians of lost secrets, seemed to watch over these underground archives, motionless witnesses to forgotten events. A chill ran down Gabriel's spine as a cold breath brushed his neck, as elusive as the ghosts of the past that seemed to be awakening around him. An invisible force seemed to trace the lines printed on the old parchments, revealing with subtle touches a complex web woven by forgotten hands.

Gabriel's thoughts wavered between fascination and apprehension. At the same time, the incessant beating of his heart imposed a breathless rhythm on his quest for truth. Suddenly, a low rumbling filled the room, vibrating like an ancient curse disturbing the present. Gabriel felt overwhelmed by a wave of invisible presences, like an audience of spectres and dark guardians emerging from the darkness to protect the priceless secrets revealed by his research. The whispered words of an ancient prophecy set his mind ablaze, instilling a sense of desperate urgency:

"Heed the warning, seeker of knowledge, for the guardians unseen may turn upon thee shouldst thou unravel their mysteries."

Torn between the magnetic pull of the ancient archives and a growing fear of unleashing an immutable wrath, Gabriel felt an irrepressible desire to pierce the veil of time and honour the memory of those whose actions echoed in the sealed silence of the crypts. He knew that the road to truth was fraught with formidable obstacles. Still, he could not look away from the exhilarating quest that lay before him, unaware of the consequences that lay ahead in the impenetrable darkness.

# 2
# The First Pieces Of The Puzzle

The reading room was shrouded in darkness. Gabriel and Dr. Fournier had sorted through the old manuscripts one by one, observing the mysterious contents of each letter written long ago with a mixture of excitement and fear. But it was in a sealed envelope, hidden between two dusty volumes, that they made their most intriguing discovery: yellowed parchments, ancient texts with enigmatic symbols, and pages stained with centuries-old ink.

The overwhelming sensation of touching history washed over them, as if these ancient writings had been whispering secrets to them for centuries. Each word revealed a forgotten piece of the past, each line held a fragment of buried truth. Time seemed to expand, freezing the moment in a bubble where the hushed atmosphere of the library mingled with the excitement of discovery. The voices of ancestors seemed to echo, whispering stories that only these manuscripts could share. Each page revealed a piece of the puzzle, prompting Gabriel and Dr. Fournier to feverishly continue their research.

The ancient inkwells exhaled an old-fashioned fragrance, reminding these modern researchers that they were the heirs to ancestral knowledge. Contemplating these manuscripts awakened in them an insatiable curiosity, a burning desire to unravel the mysteries that surrounded them. Each document seemed to hold the keys to buried knowledge, and each page turned brought them a little closer to the hidden truth. They were on the verge of uncovering a thousand-year-old secret, of bringing buried stories to life, of shedding light on forgotten corridors of history. In this silent, solemn room, time lost all meaning, giving way to a timeless adventure.

The mysterious manuscripts opened the doors to a forgotten world, inspiring Gabriel and Dr. Fournier with an urgent need to explore the twists and turns of the past. And so they continued their fascinating exploration, turning pages, uncovering words, and revealing secrets.

The atmosphere in the room was thick with dust and mystery. The shelves creaked under the weight of ancient volumes, as if they contained secrets too heavy for such old shelves to bear. Gabriel and Dr. Fournier cautiously approached the dark wooden shelves, lighting their way in the darkness with a dusty lantern. Each step seemed to awaken the muffled whispers of the past, the voices of ancestors demanding justice. The buried library, hidden behind thick walls, held the remnants of a troubled time, a time when words were weapons and ideas were dangerous. The forgotten tomes seemed to have been waiting for centuries, their weathered leather covers bearing witness to the passing years.

Old yellowed parchments mingled with worn bindings, forming a delightfully archaic amalgam of occult knowledge. Forbidden writings, subversive theories, and revolutionary ideas lay dormant within these pages, waiting for curious eyes to rediscover them and unleash their power.

The library was a tomb of knowledge, preserving the legacy of those who had dared to challenge the conventions of their time. As they made their way further in, Gabriel noticed a shelf whose wood was more worn than the others. A slight shift revealed the existence of a secret passage.

Carefully moving the books that concealed it, they discovered the entrance to a hidden room, an enclave forgotten by the outside world. Their hearts pounding, they entered this forgotten sanctuary, where a treasure trove of forbidden knowledge lay waiting. The shelves of this new room were laden with ancient manuscripts, some of which bore the distinctive mark of a family seal familiar to Gabriel.

Among these diaries signed 'A.D.,' traces of a past life and intimate reflections offered a fascinating glimpse into the history of Gabriel's ancestor. Each page turned revealed a fragment of his heritage, shedding light on the mystery of their transgenerational connection. Immersed in reading these writings, Gabriel and Dr. Fournier realised that these engraved words bore witness to the struggles and hopes of a distant era. They were transported to a world where ideas were beacons in the darkness, where the pen was often a weapon more formidable than a sword. These precious writings held the keys to their quest, promising to lift the veil on mysteries buried for generations.

Dr Fournier, illuminated by the flickering candlelight, carefully gathered the diaries signed "A.D." that she had found in the occult library. These precious manuscripts revealed a treasure trove of coded information, confidences hidden in a maze of thoughts and mysterious symbols. Gabriel watched, eager to pierce the veil separating the present from the past, his eyes lingering on each word written with captivating precision.

As silence enveloped the shadow-filled room, A.D.'s words seemed to whisper to Gabriel a story that had been waiting to be told for generations. A breath of the past seemed to rise from the yellowed pages, carrying the muffled echoes of a distant era. Each line echoed the anonymous author's ardent desire to pass on a legacy, a clear-sighted message for future generations. In a whirlwind of emotions, Gabriel was overcome by this revealing discovery. This infinitely precious find went far beyond mere personal confessions; it held the secrets of a bygone era, whose intrigues and conspiracies would certainly illuminate the dark path he was now walking.

As Dr. Fournier scrutinised the writings with methodical acuity, Gabriel let his mind wander through the twists and turns of the revelations before him. As the confessions took shape, a feeling of intimate connection with A.D. took hold of him, highlighting the inexorable convergence between his own destiny and that of this mysterious ancestor. Suddenly, a flash of blinding clarity pierced the veil of confusion surrounding the recent discoveries. Everything fit together: the hidden plans, the engraved symbols, the missing documents. The tenuous thread of time seemed to weave a complex web connecting the past and the present, awakening in Gabriel the certainty that his destiny was intimately linked to that of A.D. The power of these revelations left him speechless. Still, he was now driven by an unshakeable conviction: the truth that had been buried for centuries would soon be revealed.

The clandestine circle, a haven of freedom and rebellion against oppression, called Aurélien to carry out his first mission. It was a dark evening, shrouded in mystery, with shadows dancing on the ancient walls of Paris. The young man felt both deep apprehension and bubbling excitement as he thought about the magnitude of his task. All around him, the murmurs of the city faded away, leaving only the pounding of his own heart. Éléonore, his beloved sister and protector, had shown palpable concern when she whispered grave warnings in his ear. Despite her warnings, he felt invested in a sacred mission, a destiny that bound him intimately to this ancestral circle.

The leader of the circle, an enigmatic and wise figure, had entrusted him with a most delicate task. Aurélien had to find a subtle way to distribute the group's secret writings to sow the seeds of intellectual rebellion. He carried on his shoulders the weight of a crucial mission, one that would place him at the heart of the struggle for freedom of thought and expression.

Night became his ally as he moved stealthily through the thick darkness of the narrow alleys, slipping like a shadow among the sleeping figures. Every corner of the city now held mysteries and unsuspected dangers. His steps led him to a place as gloomy as it was majestic, a sanctuary hidden beneath the City of Light. Entering this underground place, lit only by a few flickering candles, Aurélien felt the thrill of history itself. Dusty ancient parchments, passionate and forbidden texts, a whole legacy of past and future struggles lay before him. This mission was no longer just a burden, but the promise of radical change. The words reverently engraved on these yellowed pages vibrated like shards of truth in the surrounding darkness.

Aurélien grasped the magnitude of his responsibility in the face of this subversive literature, these ideas capable of changing the course of events. The night advanced inexorably, plunging him into a state of excited and feverish wakefulness. The fateful hour was approaching, and with it the moment to let his subversive music resound through the winding streets of the sleeping capital.

Encouraged by the immortal voices of all those who had fought for freedom, Aurélien took up his pen with unwavering determination. He sketched the first notes of his rebellious symphony, capturing the essence of his hopes and aspirations, engraving the burning breath of his commitment on paper. Each musical phrase was imbued with resistance, each harmony a pacifist declaration of war.

As he completed his visionary work, Aurélien

felt an indescribable aura hovering over him, like a whisper from a time long gone. His music contained the very spirit of freedom, heralding a new era in which thought would no longer have to fear oppression. Thus, the clandestine circle became part of the grand narrative of history, through musical accents that would resonate long after their creation, carrying with them eternal hope.

It was a mild and cosy evening, with candlelight dancing on the stone walls. Éléonore, dressed in a dark velvet dress, was waiting for her brother Aurélien in the small living room of their ancestral home. The crackling of the fire in the fireplace accompanied her anxious thoughts. In that suspended moment, a glimmer of apprehension clouded her azure eyes. When Aurélien entered the room, his face was filled with a determination she had never seen in him before. He had just received his first mission from the secret society. Éléonore knew that this night would mark a turning point in their lives. She stood up, took a few steps toward her brother, and tenderly took his hands in hers.

"Aurélien, my life is in your hands tonight," she whispered, her voice tinged with emotion. "Promise me you'll be careful. These men will stop at nothing to protect their secrets."

Éléonore's words hung in the air like a veiled warning. She knew only too well the dangers that awaited those who dared to challenge the established order. The members of the clandestine circle risked their lives for ideals that seemed, rightly, to threaten the interests of the powerful. She feared for her brother, for her own safety, but also for the unpredictable consequences that Aurélien's actions might trigger.

As they exchanged a final glance before Aurélien's departure, Éléonore silently relit a candle in a gesture of prayer. Shadows danced on the walls, as if to better represent the dangers that lay ahead. She took a deep breath, trying to dispel the anxiety that gripped her heart. At that moment, a certainty dawned on her: their destiny was now set in motion, caught up in an irreversible spiral, marked by the seal of secrecy and resistance. As she returned to her room, the weight of buried secrets seemed to weigh more heavily on her delicate shoulders. She promised herself, with the quiet strength of determined souls, to watch over her brother and preserve the fragile fragments of their existence. For in the darkness of that starry night, Éléonore sensed that the veil covering their lives would soon be torn away, revealing the unsuspected cruelty and beauty of the world around them.

In the icy darkness of the library, Gabriel and Dr. Fournier pored over ancient manuscripts, searching for clues lost in the mists of time. The yellowed pages exuded a scent of the past, mingled with dust that seemed to have witnessed centuries passing by. Among these forgotten treasures, a revelation suddenly emerged: pages were missing, as if torn out by an invisible hand seeking to conceal buried truths. Gabriel felt a shiver run down his spine as Dr. Fournier shone an oil lamp into a dark corner where these precious writings had once lain. The lost words and erased paragraphs seemed to cry out about their past existence, leaving an indelible mark on the fate of those who had once put them on paper. He then realised that this subtle theft was much more than a simple theft of archives: it was an act intended to conceal a deeply buried truth, a conspiracy meticulously orchestrated through the ages.

Meanwhile, in another corner of Paris, the wind whispered ancient secrets into the ears of Aurélien Desmoulins. His mission within the clandestine circle was taking shape, and he felt the weight of the stakes resting on his shoulders. Éléonore, his vigilant sister, stood by his side, warning him of the dangers that lay ahead. But even her warnings could not dim the mysterious glow of the enigma unfolding before the young man, drawing him into a whirlwind of plots and challenges.

For hours on end, Gabriel immersed himself in these disturbing discoveries, trying to piece together the puzzle scattered by fate. He realised that these archivists of the past had foreseen, centuries ago, that their words might one day be haunted by the menacing shadow of oblivion. And yet, an undeniable connection revealed itself in these absences painted on the parchment, like an indelible signature left by fate.

As the pages turned, an ancestral truth gradually emerged, echoing the confidences whispered between the cracked walls of the Opera House. Gabriel felt an invisible force binding him to this mysterious ancestor, as if fate were skilfully weaving the fabric of their lives across the ages. The stolen archives turned out to be the invisible links connecting the chains of history, offering a thread of Ariadne in this labyrinth of unsuspected mysteries.

As Gabriel inspected the stolen archives, his gaze was drawn to an old parchment, almost hidden under a pile of dusty documents. He unfolded it carefully, revealing enigmatic inscriptions and ancient symbols that seemed to form a hidden map. Dr Fournier looked closely at this discovery, emphasising its potential importance in unravelling the mystery that surrounded them. As they examined the parchment in more detail, a glimmer of hope lit up in their eyes, for they sensed that these lost clues and clues could lead them to the truth that had been buried for centuries.

At that time, Aurélien stood before a hidden door, nervous but determined to accomplish his first mission within the clandestine circle. Éléonore, aware of the dangers that awaited her brother, offered him her last words of advice, filled with concern. Kissing an object hanging from her necklace, she whispered words of protection and encouragement, hoping that the power of the amulet would keep him safe from the dangers that lay ahead.

Meanwhile, Gabriel and Dr. Fournier continued their investigation, thinking back to the diaries signed "A.D." These accounts of the past, a mixture of passion, intrigue, and secrets, seemed to resonate mysteriously with current events, as if the link between the eras remained alive through the words and actions of their ancestors.

After long hours spent scrutinising every detail of the ancient writings, a sudden revelation struck Gabriel's mind. The dates, places, and names mentioned in the journals curiously overlapped with the information gleaned from the stolen archives. A pattern slowly emerged, as if the mysteries of the past were echoing in the present, inviting Gabriel to pierce the veil of time and reveal the buried secrets.

It was a disturbing, indescribable connection that vibrated at the heart of their every move, guiding them toward a deeper understanding of the complex web woven across the centuries. As the setting sun painted the sky with shades of purple, Gabriel realised that these lost traces and clues were much more than mere historical artefacts. They were the key to a thousand-year-old legacy, bearing forgotten stories and intertwined destinies, ready to be unveiled to the modern world. The promising glow of this discovery now lit their path, dissolving the darkness that had veiled so many truths. And as the shadows stretched into the corners of the secret library, a spark of hope shone in Gabriel's eyes, confident that each lost clue brought them inexorably closer to the ultimate truth they were striving to uncover.

In the hushed atmosphere of the library, Gabriel and Dr. Fournier had immersed themselves in the study of the mysterious manuscripts. Each parchment revealed an unsuspected piece of family history, weaving an imperceptible link between Gabriel and his ancestor A.D. The yellowed pages exuded an evocative scent, revealing the well-kept secrets of a bygone era. As Gabriel fervently deciphered the esoteric symbols adorning the ancient pages, a revelation dawned on him. These writings concealed the beginnings of a long-buried story, which he was destined to unravel. Dr. Fournier, herself captivated by the spellbinding aura of these discoveries, sensed in Gabriel an unexpected drive, a quest for truth that transcended the limits of time.

Meanwhile, in a dark alley in 19th-century Paris, Aurélien stepped through the first doors of the clandestine circle. Éléonore, alert and far-sighted, had conveyed her fears to him with concern tinged with anxiety. The two eras seemed to echo each other, as if the thread of history bent space and time to connect these destinies separated by centuries.

Distant echoes reached Gabriel, who understood that every action of his ancestor still resonated today, in the turmoil of the present.

A sense of urgency overwhelmed him, driving him to find the keys hidden in these timeless manuscripts to untangle the knots that bound their souls together. The breath of the past caressed the contours of the secret, whispering to Gabriel fragments of a truth stifled by oblivion. He sensed that behind each word scribbled by A.D. lay the indelible imprint of a vivid legacy, a legacy of which he was the unwitting but determined guardian.

The darkness of the library was disturbed by this revelation, bathing the two researchers in a new light. The veils of time were torn away, revealing subtle links between the Desmoulins of yesteryear and Gabriel, their descendant. Aurélien's image superimposed itself on his, calling out to him across the ages to take part in the immutable dance of history. At the heart of this silent symphony, a certainty emerged: the pieces of the puzzle, scattered across generations, formed a single picture, the contours of which gradually took shape in Gabriel's mind, eager for answers.

Silence hung heavily in the room, as if laden with the suffering and hopes that echoed through the ages. Gabriel and Dr. Fournier sat in front of the secret bookcase, immersed in silent contemplation of the diaries signed "A.D."

It was a moment of almost palpable intensity, a moment when the weight of centuries seemed to rest on their shoulders. The yellowed pages exuded a scent of mystery, and the calligraphic words seemed to whisper deeply buried truths. The passages evoked a time when ideas were bubbling, when fiery passions clashed with the darkness of oppression. Each word was a window onto a lost world, a world where a man named Aurélien Desmoulins burned with a fiery passion for justice and freedom. In these writings, Gabriel sensed the distant echo of the battles fought by his own ancestor. This echo strangely resonated in his tormented heart.

Meanwhile, as Gabriel and Dr. Fournier pored over these precious manuscripts, in another time, Aurélien nervously paced the worn cobblestones of a dark alley. Éléonore, his beloved sister, had warned him of the dangers that awaited those who dared to challenge the powers that be. And yet, despite the fears that crept into his heart, he felt deep within himself the urgent call to action. His mission within the clandestine circle was the spark that fuelled the flame of his determination.

The discovery of this secret library was not only the revelation of a hidden treasure, but an open door to a parallel universe, a complex web of intertwined destinies. These writings brought back the thoughts and emotions of a troubled era, weaving an unbreakable link between the past and the present. Gabriel could feel this link vibrating within him, capable of transcending the barriers of time and space. He was now certain that vital documents had been stolen from the archives, documents that could shed light on the grey areas surrounding the heroic deeds he had found echoing in Aurélien Desmoulins' journals.

As the shadow of the past enveloped their tormented minds, a powerful connection slowly crystallised, like the filaments of an invisible network connecting generations. An irresistible force drove them to continue their quest, to follow this tortuous path marked by events buried in the bowels of history. What unspeakable secret lay behind these ancient writings, what coded message was hidden beneath the words worn away by time? Their hearts pounded with the knowledge that the answer lay in a passage to the past, where forgotten heroes waited patiently to be rescued from oblivion.

Darkness enveloped Gabriel and Camille as they entered the tunnel hidden beneath the Opera House. Their lamp illuminated walls covered with mysterious symbols, seeming to whisper forgotten stories. They moved cautiously, as if afraid of awakening secrets that had been dormant for centuries. In their hands, they held the diaries of A.D., whose yellowed pages revealed thoughts and experiences from another time. Each word seemed to pulsate like the heart of their ancestor, guiding them through the twists and turns of history.

Suddenly, the smell of old parchment enveloped them, and they discovered a hidden library filled with ancient books. The words on the covers seemed to vibrate with a special energy, as if they had been waiting for generations for someone to unlock their mysteries. Among these dusty volumes, Gabriel found a book that contained the teachings of the secret circle, forbidden knowledge that had been carefully preserved.

Meanwhile, as Gabriel and Camille were immersed in this world of the past, another scene was unfolding in parallel. Aurélien, Gabriel's distant ancestor, was receiving his first mission within the secret circle. Éléonore, his sister, watched him with concern, knowing that this step into the shadows could change the course of their destiny forever. She had always watched over him, fearing the dangers that awaited those who dared to defy convention. The two timelines seemed to converge in a silent dialogue, weaving invisible links between the eras.

Old 19th-century manuscripts in Gabriel's

hands were the keys to a hidden door to the past, connecting the present to a forgotten world. He now understood that documents had been removed from the archives to hide the truth, but he was determined to shed light on these buried secrets. As they made their way through the tunnel, a shiver ran through Gabriel, as if he could feel the benevolent presence of those who had lived before him.

Soon, the path would reveal its mysteries, and the echoes of the past would be heard, revealing truths buried in the shadows. An invisible connection was forming between the protagonists of the past and present, as if to remind them that the course of history never ends, but continues through time, connecting the daring souls who dare to listen to its story.

# 3

# The Web Is Woven

Gabriel went to the Parisian café, a charming place steeped in an old-fashioned atmosphere. The chandeliers flickered dimly, enveloping the guests in a soft light that added to the mysterious aura of the place. When he spotted the descendant of the Count of Beaumont sitting at a table in the back, he felt a palpable tension rise in the air, as if fate itself had woven an invisible web around them. The man was elegantly dressed, his piercing gaze seeming to peer into Gabriel's soul. They exchanged polite greetings, but every word was weighed with calculated caution.

The Count's descendant expressed veiled concerns about Gabriel's research, suggesting that certain secrets should remain buried for the good of all. His words were laden with innuendo, leaving a vague aura of menace hanging in the air. Yet, Gabriel did not allow himself to be intimidated. He sensed that his investigation would reveal essential truths, truths that had been hidden for too long. He resisted with quiet resolve, refusing to bow to the descendant's manipulations. Each of his replies was tinged with determination, as if the past itself were speaking through him, demanding justice for those who had been forgotten by history.

The café seemed suspended in time, frozen

in a timeless moment where the fates of these two men were inexorably intertwined. Through the windows, the last rays of the setting sun bathed the room in a golden glow, adding a touch of melancholy to the solemn scene. The muffled murmurs of the other customers seemed distant, as if the outside world had faded away, leaving room for a silent tête-à-tête laden with unspoken meanings.

The meeting ended on an uncertain note. Their eyes met one last time, and each knew that this confrontation was only the prelude to future revelations. As Gabriel left the café, he felt something new awakening within him: an unwavering determination to continue his quest for the truth, no matter what dark shadows loomed in his path. In the hushed atmosphere of a richly decorated room, Gabriel found himself face to face with the descendant of the Count of Beaumont.

The man, with his refined bearing and piercing gaze, exuded an aura of intrigue and mystery. From their first exchanges, Gabriel felt a palpable tension, as if every word spoken had a hidden weight, with undertones concealed in the polite words. The Count's descendant, in a soft, measured voice, attempted to shake Gabriel's resolve. He used subtle tricks to sow doubt in the historian's mind, evoking the dire consequences that could result from continuing his investigations. Veiled allusions to secrets buried for generations were skilfully woven into the conversation, sowing confusion in Gabriel's mind.

Yet despite his interlocutor's elegant persuasion, Gabriel remained unyielding. His sharp, analytical mind discerned the pretence behind the polite bows. He sensed the insidious manoeuvres being plotted in the shadows by this man whose interests conflicted with his own. The room, a silent witness to this verbal confrontation, seemed to hold its breath, captivated by the stakes of this verbal joust.

Shadows danced on the walls, as if to emphasise the intensity of this clash between two stubborn wills. The Count's descendant, seeing that his tactics of dissuasion were not having the desired effect, opted for a more direct approach. His words became sharper, his insinuations less veiled. He evoked the honour of his lineage and the need to preserve certain buried truths, while allowing the subtle shadow of disguised blackmail to linger.

Faced with this implicit threat, Gabriel felt his nerves tense, but a fierce determination lit up his eyes. He knew that pursuing the quest for truth involved risks, but backing down in the face of these veiled threats would have been a betrayal of his ancestors' memory. Thus, in this room where the stakes were subtly intertwined, the confrontation between the rival descendants proved to be much more complex than their seemingly courteous encounter had suggested.


The Count of Beaumont's gaze scrutinised Éléonore with disturbing intensity. During the masked ball held in the dazzling opulence of his home, she felt as if she were being watched, spied on, perhaps even judged. Yet behind her sophisticated mask, she struggled to hide her true feelings, trying to appear carefree, even though every beat of her heart betrayed her anxiety. Already troubled by recent events and the secret preparations of the clandestine group, Éléonore felt the weight of responsibility on her frail shoulders. She was aware that she played a crucial role in the plot to expose the truth and challenge the established order.

Yet, the Count's menacing presence continued to sow doubt in her mind. A cold smile appeared on the Count's face as he approached Éléonore, mingling with the elegant crowd that waltzed gracefully to the enchanting sound of the orchestra. His deep, cold voice rang in her ear, whispering honeyed words tinged with menace. He reminded her of her place in the world, her status as a woman, vulnerable at any moment to being crushed by the relentless wheels of power and manipulation. Clenching her fists beneath the silky folds of her shimmering dress, Éléonore refused to give in to the terror that threatened to overwhelm her. She thought of her brother, Aurélien, and their shared commitment to truth and justice. It was this deep conviction that gave her the courage to hold the Count's imperious gaze, despite the fear that gripped her heart.

Meanwhile, in the present, Gabriel felt a chill of unease, unable to explain precisely the reason for his discomfort. The encounter with the descendant of the Count of Beaumont had deeply disturbed him, fuelling his insatiable curiosity and strengthening his determination to probe the mysteries of the past. Aware that dark forces were seeking to hinder his quest, he vowed to continue his investigations at all costs, despite the veiled threats and urgent warnings. The web seemed to be thickening around him, but he knew deep in his soul that he had to untangle the threads of the mystery so that the truth could finally emerge.

The whirling dance echoed through the vast hall of the castle. The chandeliers sparkled, illuminating the shimmering masks of the guests. Everything was luxury and splendour, but behind the facade lay hidden intrigues and unspoken ambitions. Éléonore, dressed in an elegant gown with a train, moved gracefully among the high society, hiding her turmoil behind a mask of determination. However, an imposing presence in the shadows caught her attention.

The Count of Beaumont, a skilled manipulator with a charming smile, eyed each guest like a cat watching its prey. His piercing eyes fell on Éléonore, sending an imperceptible shiver down her spine. She knew that her mistrust of the clandestine group was growing, and that her every move was being scrutinised by the Count.

The intoxicating melodies of the orchestra seemed to drown out the whispers of conspiracy that hung in the air. Éléonore felt the weight of the evening pressing down on her frail shoulders, but she had to remain faithful to her mission. Despite the oppression that gripped her heart, she wore a radiant smile, sparkling behind her black velvet mask.

The Count suddenly approached her, like a predator stalking its prey. His magnetic gaze seemed to pierce through the fabric of Éléonore's dress, revealing her most intimate thoughts. Every word he uttered was laced with flattery and manipulation. He exerted a poisonous seduction over her, seeking to probe her convictions and sow doubt in her mind.

Despite her feigned confidence, Éléonore felt

the tension rising within her. She had to remain impassive, guardian of the precious secrets her heart held. Amidst this masquerade of appearances, she knew that the real battle was being fought in the subtle nuances of the exchanges between the guests. Every dance step, every formal exchange, was a pawn on the chessboard of a silent struggle for freedom and justice. While masks veiled faces, the truth remained elusive, harbouring dangers and promises. Éléonore resisted, like a rose blooming among the thorns of conspiracy. She had to stay strong, aware that every moment spent under the Count's gaze brought her a little closer to the inevitable outcome of their confrontation.

The masked ball scene unfolds like a complex dance between masks and true intentions. The sparkling chandeliers cast a soft light, illuminating faces hidden behind sumptuous masks. It is impossible to say whether the magnificence of the finery rivals the sparkle in the eyes, where the best-kept secrets can be glimpsed. The guests move forward, draped in opulent attire, while the murmurs of the music fill the atmosphere with mystery. In this whirlwind of pretence, each step reveals a game of deception, and the dance of the masks hides unsuspected enigmas. At the bend in an aisle, the Count of Beaumont appears, majestic beneath his chiselled silver mask, escorting Éléonore, whose scarlet dress seems to burn with a thousand lights. His gaze seems to navigate between determination and concern, capturing all the subtlety of their silent exchanges. Behind his impenetrable mask, the Count makes veiled promises, while Éléonore stifles her fears to serve the common cause.

Meanwhile, in the shadows of the hushed alcoves, other figures are swept away by the waltz of appearances. Aurélien, his heart full of confidence, holds out a glimmer of hope. At the same time, Raphaël, tormented by jealousy, seems ready to betray the unthinkable.

The conspiracy slowly takes shape, through whispered phrases and plots hatched in secret. Every laugh, every sigh, hints at fragile alliances and latent betrayals. The secret action takes shape, imperceptibly, under the mask of propriety. Complicit glances are exchanged, and ambiguous gestures light up the dark corridors.

At the same time, passion, the blind guide of intertwined destinies, plays with convention. The murmurs of the conspirators mingle with the spellbinding music, weaving the invisible threads that bind history to the audacity of a few. In this masked ball, the stakes go beyond mere worldly entertainment: it is a struggle against obscurantism, to liberate thought and affirm the aspiration for freedom, where only the courageous dare to brave the masks.

The tension was palpable, seeming to float in the atmosphere like a dark veil ready to fall. Gabriel felt a mixture of excitement and apprehension at the turn of events. As the descendant of the Count of Beaumont tried to sow doubt in his mind, a fierce determination took hold of him, driving him to unravel the mysteries of the past at any cost.

Meanwhile, in the twists and turns of history, the clandestine group gathered in secret to plot a political action that would change the course of events forever. Alliances were formed, plans were woven like a complex web where each thread had to be handled with care so as not to reveal their purpose. In the shadows, conspirators exchanged furtive glances, whispering words laden with meaning. Hearts beat in unison, bearing the weight of their plans, while the future lay in their hands. Fear and excitement intermingled, creating an electric atmosphere conducive to the awakening of dormant consciences. Éléonore, a young woman with a lively temperament and sharp intelligence, stood at the heart of this secret action, ready to defy convention to serve her cause. Her eyes shone with unwavering determination, revealing an unsuspected strength that made her captivating.

Meanwhile, in the present, Gabriel was forging unshakeable resolutions, refusing to bow to the veiled threats of Beaumont's descendant. His research had become a personal quest, transcending the simple desire for knowledge to embrace an urgent duty to his ancestors. With every page turned, every clue deciphered, he drew closer to the truth that had been buried for so many years. Secret action was brewing in the shadows, like a master stroke on the chessboard of fate, ready to be revealed in a final coup de théâtre. The suspense, vibrating with promise and revelation, hung in the air, promising to unveil long-buried truths and destinies linked by the thread of time.

As night spread its dark veil over the sleeping city, Gabriel summoned his courage in the face of the Count of Beaumont's descendants' machinations. Driven by unwavering determination, he categorically refused to give in to the fear sown by the stratagems and lies concocted to hinder his quest for truth.

Under the soft glow of the streetlights, he found himself caught up in a relentless struggle between the forces of the past, embodied by these descendants thirsty for buried secrets, and his insatiable thirst to uncover the reality that had been hidden for generations. Every fibre of his being vibrated with the rhythm of his unyielding resolve, guiding his steps toward the fulfilment of his destiny, intertwined with that of his ancestors.

The descendant of Beaumont, filled with resentment and confusion, attempted through many treacherous tricks to sow doubt in Gabriel's mind, hoping to dissuade him from exploring the mysteries of the past mixed with the present. However, like a rock battered by the raging waves of adversity, Gabriel stood firm, nurturing the burning flame of perseverance in his heart. His steps led him to closed doors, silent guardians of ancient mysteries. Still, no obstacle could contain the inner strength that animated his soul. In this tense confrontation, the shadows of the past danced in Gabriel's eyes, projecting reflections of an immutable history, ready to reveal itself under his impetus.

Facing the turmoil of uncertainty, he embraced the memory of his ancestors, imbuing himself with their audacity and resilience, which filled the atmosphere of that moment frozen in time. Each obstacle in his path only galvanised his determination, transforming every trap into a challenge to be overcome and every detour into an opportunity to thwart the sinister plans hatched against him. Thus, on that night shrouded in mystery, Gabriel advanced like an intrepid scout, guided by the flickering light of truth that illuminated his tortuous path. His mind was clad in the armour of his heroism, and his thoughts soared like a grand symphony, carried by the sincerity of his commitment to the memory of his predecessors. This indestructible determination sealed his fate to that of the heroes of the past, binding their lives forever in a common quest, tinged with glimmers of hope and promises of redemption.

The descendant of the Count of Beaumont, a man with a haughty demeanour and ambiguous words, tried by every means to sow doubt in Gabriel's mind. His stratagems were as subtle as they were pernicious, wrapped in a carefully woven web of lies. Every word uttered by this man seemed to be tinged with a sly venom, aimed at shaking Gabriel's resolve.

Despite his efforts to conceal his true intentions, the fleeting glint of malice in his eyes betrayed the devious nature of his designs. His cunning speech oscillated between a desire to dissuade Gabriel from continuing his research and an apparent fear that the dreaded truth would come to light. Gabriel found himself at the centre of a verbal joust where every word was weighed and every gesture scrutinised. He could clearly see that behind the hushed appearances of politeness lay treacherous manoeuvres, hatched in the shadows of dark designs from the past.

Meanwhile, in the depths of the 19th century, the clandestine group was secretly preparing a significant political action. The whispers of the ancient walls carried the echoes of their nightly meetings, resonating like discordant notes floating in the thick air of conspiracy. As the days passed, Éléonore, while remaining the focus of the Count's attention, used ingenious tricks to conceal the activities of her brother Aurélien and their accomplices.

The game of appearances orchestrated at the masked ball, where masks served as much to hide faces as to conceal subversive designs, took a perilous turn. The plot thickened, with the protagonists playing with the limits of deception and loyalty. Confrontations took place as much in the fashionable salons as in the underground labyrinths, where secrets rumbled like storms ready to break. The hour was approaching when stratagems and lies would be laid bare, revealing the naked truth in all its troubled splendour.

The masked ball had come to an end, leaving behind an atmosphere tinged with mystery and preparation. In the silent corridors of the Opera House, the whispers of the ancient walls seemed to intensify, as if announcing the secrets they held. Gabriel felt the weight of history bearing down on his shoulders, but his determination remained unshakeable. As he searched the dusty archives for clues, the shadows of the past seemed to come to life, revealing fragments of a troubled era. The yellowed pages of diaries signed "A.D." seemed to vibrate beneath his fingers, transmitting the intense emotions of his ancestor. As darkness gradually enveloped the sleeping Opera House, Gabriel found himself in a state of deep meditation. Forgotten passions seemed to echo within him, bringing forth a wave of courage to face the adversity that lay ahead. The whispers of the ancient walls evoked past struggles and sacrifices, and exuded the promise of an imminent revelation.

Through the twists and turns of time, he could hear the distant echoes of the political action fomented by the clandestine group, while the plans of Beaumont's descendant took shape like menacing spectres ready to haunt his path. Yet beyond the dark designs, Gabriel also discerned a glimmer of hope and resistance. Éléonore, an emblematic figure from the past, seemed to transcend the centuries to convey her strength and determination to him. Her sparkling eyes and daring actions echoed in the austere opulence of the deserted halls, reminding Gabriel that the choice of courage was now his. Faced with the challenges ahead, Gabriel knew that the whispers of the ancient walls only strengthened his resolve. In the echoes of voices past, he discovered the elusive melody of heroism and justice, inviting him to embrace his destiny with the fierce determination of an heir aware of the importance of his legacy. So, reinvigorated by the call of history, he prepared to face the darkness and ensure the triumph of the flame of truth, in the name of those whose whispers remained eternal within the ancient walls of the Opera House.

Gabriel found himself at a crossroads, overwhelmed by the disturbing revelations and veiled threats that surrounded him. In the suffocating darkness of the corridors, he felt the almost tangible weight of ancestral history bearing down on his shoulders, as if every ancient stone were trying to whisper a discreet warning. Despite the constant assaults aimed at breaking his resolve, a glimmer of daring awakened within him, fuelled by the memory of the unsung heroes of the past, ready to brave adversity in pursuit of the truth. As the descendant of the Count of Beaumont persisted in his attempts to dissuade him, deploying refined tricks and poisonous words, Gabriel refused to bow to the darkness that sought to close in on him. Every cold glance, every calculated smile, only strengthened his resolve, fuelling an inner flame of fearlessness. His mind was imbued with the heroic stories of his ancestor, haloed with bravery and sacrifice, and he vowed to follow in their footsteps with the same recklessness.

Meanwhile, in the veiled world of the 19th century, the members of the clandestine group were fine-tuning their strategy, aware that every move they made was a battle against oppression and injustice. Éléonore, a figure as enigmatic as she was admirable, was confronted with the unpleasant advances of the Count of Beaumont, but remained unyielding in her determination to protect the ideals for which she fought. Through the prism of time, her actions echoed the steadfastness Gabriel showed in his own present struggle, creating an unbreakable bond between these two distinct eras.

The masked ball of appearances and fallen masks gradually revealed the stakes of a battle that transcended the limits of time. Secret action was brewing in the shadows of both eras, invisibly weaving the threads of destiny together in an inextricable web. In this underground dance between past and present, each hesitant step became a promise of courage, each secret revealed a proclamation of integrity.

Finally, immersed in this universe of intertwined temporal layers, Gabriel fully embraced his perilous mission with renewed strength. He knew that every lie exposed, every stratagem foiled, only strengthened his unshakeable conviction that the truth could not be silenced. And while the whispers of the ancient walls seemed to murmur warnings, they actually fuelled his determination, whispering that the choice of courage was the only one worth making.

# 4
# Art In Resistance

The Opera archives were overflowing with old scores, silent witnesses to the melodies of the past. Accompanied by darkness and silence, Gabriel began his quest in this ocean of frozen notes. His fingers brushing the yellowed parchments, he scrutinised every line, every sign, searching for a secret echo of the past. It was in the precision of the annotations, almost erased by time, that the key to this musical enigma might lie. Like an archaeologist faced with ancient runes, he examined each measure, searching for the harmony hidden beneath the surface.

Slowly, a revelation began to dawn: unusual patterns were hidden in the score, symbols concealed between the eighth notes and half notes, a cryptic language woven into the musical fabric. Each note became imbued with secret meaning, each pause a moment laden with mystery. His hands, as if guided by an invisible force, gradually revealed a coded message that would transcend time and space. The music suddenly came to life, vibrating with unexpected nuances.

In this parallel universe revealed by the scores, Aurélien's work took on a new dimension, reconfiguring the present in the light of its past. The score became a bridge between two eras, a timeless link connecting Gabriel to the destiny of his ancestor. Each measure explored brought the thin thread separating the centuries a little closer together, making Aurélien's musical legacy tangible. Thus, immersed in this rediscovered intimacy with past virtuosity, Gabriel felt the warm embrace of successive generations, a legacy passed down through the pages of music. And it was in this harmonious intertwining of secret and revelation that Gabriel found a part of himself, revealed by the mysterious twists and turns of these ancient scores.

Aurélien, a passionate young composer, had a gift for weaving intense emotions into each of his musical creations. But this time, his inspiration went far beyond simply composing a harmonious piece.

Knowing he was being watched by members of the clandestine circle, Aurélien decided to hide secret messages within his musical work. Each note, each melodic variation was intended to convey coded information, a call to rebellion hidden in the universal language of music. With incredible ingenuity, he managed to weave these subtle messages into a spellbinding symphony, bringing to life a creation with a double meaning. On the surface, the work appeared to be an exemplary artistic composition, touching hearts and captivating minds with its sheer beauty and power. Still, in reality, it contained a hidden narrative, a story of intrigue and resistance.

Each musical movement, each crescendo, held a fragment of truth, a piece of the forbidden history that the Count was trying to silence at all costs. And it was with fierce determination that Aurélien continued his work, aware of the risk he was taking in openly defying the authorities. Éléonore, her brother's loyal ally, played a crucial role in this cover-up. She used every means at her disposal to protect Aurélien's composition, disguising the coded scores as innocent-looking sheet music. Thus, the ballroom became the silent theatre of a silent opposition, where harmonious chords hid well-kept secrets. In the glare of the chandeliers and under the weight of the masks, art transcended its primary function to become an instrument of resistance. It was in this subtle blend of beauty and concealment that Aurélien's music rose, ready to expose the truth to anyone who was able to hear it.

The musical notes seemed to dance across the score, forming an enchanting melody, but beneath this secret symphony lay much more than a simple composition. Aurélien's nimble fingers had divinely woven a complex web of codes and messages hidden within each bar. Each note, each nuance contributed to the puzzle, carefully camouflaged behind the dazzling beauty of the work. As the young man put the finishing touches to his creation, Éléonore watched in admiration as her brother brought to life a masterpiece that, far beyond his artistic reach, would be the pillar of their clandestine struggle. Without a word, she understood that this music would play a crucial role in the resistance that was forming, a weapon hidden in the innocence of the scores, ready to reveal its secrets to those in the know.

Meanwhile, in the present day, Gabriel was stunned to discover the fallout from the Count's evil plans. The direct threats he had received made it clear that his quest for the truth was not welcome. But an irrepressible force drove him on, compelling him to continue his investigations and unravel the web of mysteries that haunted him. His suspicions grew as he began to seriously consider the possibility of a link between past events and the current turmoil.

It was in this state of inner turmoil that Gabriel decided to immerse himself body and soul in the music he had inherited from Aurélien. Convinced that crucial clues were buried in the score, he set out to find the hidden message with the invaluable help of Camille. Each note, each rhythm, became a symbol to be decoded, a key to unlocking the doors of the past and understanding the insidious secret that linked these two distant eras. In the shadows of the opera house, as the scales rang out in the air thick with urgency, Gabriel sensed that this art form, stripped of its original innocence, concealed the actual stakes of a thousand-year struggle.

Music became for him the mirror of this resistance, the sublime expression of a silent but oh-so-essential war. The century-old piano, steeped in past suffering, was the last bastion where the novelist began his feverish search for the encrypted message, determined to uncover the obscure legacy left by Aurélien, a bearer of meaning and freedom. Each discovery he made was a step closer to unravelling the truth, and the weight of his findings was not lost on him.


The Count de Beaumont, a man with a haughty demeanour and a scrutinising gaze, had always been observant. His piercing eyes scrutinised the slightest movements of those around him. Since Gabriel Moreau's arrival at the Paris Opera, a growing unease had been creeping over him. From whispered conversations to exchanged glances in the wings, nothing escaped his unparalleled acuity. As the days passed, this anxiety turned to suspicion. He compared events, pieced together clues, and a sinister picture began to form in his mind. The dark corridors of the Opera House seemed to become his battlefield, where every shadow might hide a traitor or a conspirator.

Gabriel, for his part, felt the weight of this growing mistrust. Every moment spent within the walls of the Opera House was tinged with palpable tension. The furtive glances and heavy silences weighed on his shoulders like silent reproaches. Even Camille, usually so confident, seemed affected by the oppressive atmosphere. Yet, Gabriel remained determined to continue his investigation at all costs. The direct threats he had received only strengthened his resolve. He had a vague feeling that at the heart of this secret plot lay the key to many mysteries.

The rehearsals continued, but the crystalline notes rising from the scores now seemed laden with hidden meaning. Each crescendo whispered a promise of revelation, each pause rested on a well-kept secret. Art, ever watchful, became a silent witness to a thousand-year-old resistance, invisible beneath its innocent exterior. The Count redoubled his efforts to stifle any hint of rebellion, to crush any glimmer of opposition. His grip on the Opera seemed to tighten, crushing any desire for independence.

But beyond the gilded trappings and velvet curtains, an intangible force persisted, elusive and prophetic. And while musical passions mingled with hushed plots, a shared destiny, woven in the depths of history, was preparing to unfold in a final Act whose outcome no one could predict.

The musical notes danced across the worn pages of the scores, revealing secrets that had been buried for decades. Gabriel, immersed in the secret library, and Camille, accompanying him with her medical and musical expertise, patiently deciphered each stave, searching for clues hidden in the haunting melodies. They knew that music had always been a means of resistance, a way to communicate without arousing the suspicion of the oppressors. Similarly, in the past, Aurélien's symphonies were much more than simple compositions; they carried coded messages intended to rally hearts to a noble cause.

Beyond the soft tones and powerful crescendos, the music contained subtle fragments of truth. In their quest for revelation, Gabriel and Camille understood the significance of their mission, beyond the echoes of the ancient instruments that still vibrated within the mysterious opera house. The hidden music room echoed with the sounds of the past, enveloping the protagonists in an enchanting but also threatening aura. The burdens of history seemed to weigh heavily on the shoulders of the researchers in this atmosphere, where the scores concealed treasures and dangers in equal measure. The musicians of the past had breathed a rebellious spirit into their works, braving adversity through their instruments. Similarly, Éléonore had played a crucial role in hiding Aurélien's compositions in her stage costumes, thus transforming artistic performance into an act of silent defiance against oppression. Each measure of music carried within it the hope and promise of a future where freedom would triumph.

Gabriel, consumed by his passion for music and the family history intertwined with it, felt the urgency to uncover the secret buried in the old piano at the Opera House. The direct threats he had received only strengthened his determination to uncover the truth hidden in the forgotten chords. The instrument filled the room with its melancholy whispers, as if calling for help to release the stifled truths. The tension mounted as Gabriel neared the dénouement. At the same time, Camille offered solid support, ready to face the poignant revelations that the melody of the past promised to bring. The old piano had held musical secrets for too long, ready to deliver its message, the valid key to the mystery that bound together the intertwined destinies of the past and present.

At this crucial moment, Gabriel found himself facing an old piano with a chipped finish, hidden in the dusty darkness of a forgotten room in the Paris Opera House. The direct threats he had received seemed to converge on this place, as if fate had chosen this page of history to reveal its best-kept secrets. His mind was filled with electric tension as he delicately touched the faded keys of the piano, hoping to discover the slightest clue that could change the course of his investigation. Each note resonated like the whisper of a dark and mysterious past. The sweet melody that escaped from the old instrument seemed imbued with a silent urgency, as if it contained within it an essential message that only a brilliant mind would be able to decipher. Gabriel knew full well that time was running out, that every second that passed brought the enigma closer to its inevitable resolution. Immersed in a kind of melodic trance, he recalled the enigmatic symbols engraved on the old parchments, frantically searching for a musical link that might unlock the mysteries of history.

With his eyes closed, he let his fingers dance

across the keyboard, listening intently to each harmony that came to life under his inspired touch. Suddenly, a sequence of unusual notes caught his attention, as if they were the distant echo of a desperate call from a bygone era. Guided by an extraordinary intuition, Gabriel began to meticulously write down these singular notes in a dust-stained notebook, taking care to transcribe their distinctive tonality with precision. As he did so, he felt a tremendous force grip him, as if the secret vibrations of the music were drawing his mind to the outer reaches of an ancient mystery. The hours passed silently as Gabriel, engrossed in his musical quest, attempted to piece together the scattered fragments of a puzzle as old as the Opera House itself.

As night enveloped the Opera House in its ethereal cloak, Gabriel let himself be carried away by a growing passion for this coded music, exploring each complex variation with fierce determination. The shifting shadows cast spectral reflections on the wood-panelled walls, creating an unreal tableau where the present and the past seemed to merge in a ghostly dance. Far from prying eyes, in this parallel universe shaped by transcendental notes, Gabriel was ready to face any challenge, to unravel the mysteries that had defied time and to triumph over the dark forces that loomed above him.

In the darkness of the Opera House wings, a sinister presence was taking shape. Gabriel and Camille had discovered a hidden message in the old piano. Still, this breakthrough in their quest had attracted the attention of dark forces. Veiled threats materialised in the form of relentless pressure, furtive glances, and whispers that seemed to follow the two seekers at every turn. The tension was palpable as menacing shadows seemed to lurk in the dark corners of the theatre.

Meanwhile, in the memories of the 19th century, Éléonore played her role as a hidden messenger with exquisite grace. Concealing coded sheet music in the folds of her stage costumes, she became the very embodiment of artistic resistance. However, her bravery had not gone unnoticed. The Count's suspicions grew day by day, fuelled by the mystery surrounding Éléonore's musical performances. Every note, every gesture took on new meaning in this perilous chess game where the slightest mistake could lead to the discovery of the secret network. As Gabriel and Camille delved into the mysteries of music to decipher the hidden messages, they also had to fight against the dark forces that sought to keep them in the shadows behind the scenes. The enchanting beauty of the Opera was tinged with a heavy atmosphere of menace, as art became a battlefield between freedom and oppression. Each musical composition became an act of rebellion, each score a manifesto of resistance. In this context, the notes themselves seemed to resonate like calls to insurrection, whispers of truth stifled by the weight of history.

Despite the insidious threats, Gabriel and Camille persevered, clinging to the hope that light would eventually dispel the darkness. They knew that their mission was not only to uncover the truth buried in Aurélien's compositions, but also to defend the legacy of courageous artists who had chosen to stand up against injustice. Their efforts were more than just a search for a lost treasure: it was a fight to preserve the very soul of the Opera so that its music could continue to resonate as a timeless symbol of freedom. And so, in the shadows of the wings, as dark forces conspired to stop them, Gabriel and Camille closed ranks, setting the stage for a final confrontation that would bring to light not only the secrets of the past but also the unsung heroes who had fought for the truth to the rhythm of forbidden melodies.


The flickering candlelight bathed the room, casting a golden glow on the scattered sheet music. Gabriel, absorbed in his quest for the truth hidden in the music, frantically searched for clues hidden between the notes. Camille observed, casting a benevolent gaze on his friend, sharing his determination to unravel the mystery that haunted the Paris Opera.

In the past, Éléonore Desmoulins, beautiful, courageous, and remarkably intelligent, had been the secret messenger of a silent rebellion. Under the oppression of the Count of Beaumont, she had discovered that the power of words could be eclipsed by the enchanting force of music. So, accompanied by Aurélien's secret compositions, she wove coded messages, harmoniously blending notes to hide words of hope and freedom. Her graceful hand traced musical symbols imbued with courage and a desire for change, before concealing them in a score performed during a memorable performance. As the intoxicating melodies enchanted the audience, the clandestine message travelled stealthily through hearts thirsty for freedom. The growing suspicions of the Count of Beaumont only reinforced the imperceptibility of the symbols engraved in the scores, thus preserving the fragile hope that resided within the clandestine circle. Nowadays, as Gabriel scrutinised each page with feverish concentration, Camille felt a sweet melody hovering in the air, as if the breath of the past were whispering buried secrets to her. Subtle emotions mingled with determination, creating an electric atmosphere charged with anticipation. Each invisible brushstroke of Éléonore, carefully orchestrated in the ancestral silence of the Opera House, seemed to vibrate through the ages to guide Gabriel toward the truth buried at the heart of the music. A shiver ran down Gabriel's spine when he realised that the old piano, abandoned in the shadows of the wings for decades, might hold the precious musical message he was seeking. The direct threats he had received seemed to be a sinister reflection of the obstacles Éléonore had faced. Music, a symbol of resistance between the two eras, became the thread connecting the epic past to the tumultuous present. Then, as his fingers touched the faded keys of the piano, Gabriel felt a familiar vibration resonate within him. It wouldn't be long before he pierced the veil of mystery surrounding the lost score, revealing to the modern world the unsuspected power of art in resistance.

The corridors of the Opera House echo with the hurried footsteps of Gabriel and Camille as they search every nook and cranny for a hidden treasure. The frescoes adorning the walls seem to whisper ancestral secrets, while the heady scent of history fills the air. The mission that consumes them goes beyond a simple quest: it is an immersion into the very soul of the Opera. This journey transcends time and awakens the echoes of an artistic resistance entrenched in timeless scores. Every hidden note, every musical breath that escapes from the yellowed pages, promises to reveal the coveted key. Guided by their passion and fearlessness, they explore the labyrinthine maze where the splendour of the past and the mystery of the present intertwine. Far from prying eyes, under the flickering light of ancient chandeliers, they unearth the forgotten vestiges of rebellion inscribed in the symphonies. Gabriel's nimble fingers brush the fragile pages, frantically searching for traces of this true Holy Grail of a score. Every silence, every inflexion fuels the hope of an imminent discovery, pitting palpable danger against an unquenchable thirst for truth.

Meanwhile, as shadows dance to the rhythm of the torches, an electric tension emanates from the spectres of the past. The contours of the darkness reveal traces of a dark destiny that shaped the Count's conspiracies. The urgency becomes palpable, as if the fragile harmony of the present threatens to disintegrate at any moment under the weight of buried secrets. The lost score then emerges like a jewel hidden within the layers of time, a sparkling reflection laden with hope and despair. At every turn, around every corner, Gabriel and Camille continue their quest with ever-increasing fervour. Their eyes light up with fierce determination, galvanised by the conviction that the score is full of notes that carry the promise of freedom. For in these musical lines lies the story of a silent rebellion, an immortal act of resistance engraved in the very flesh of the Opera House. And as their footsteps grow more urgent and the hours melt into a feverish whirlwind, the hope of writing a new page in the history of the Opera guides them inexorably toward their destiny.

The notes rose in the darkness of the Opera House, weaving a musical drama that resonated like a declaration of independence. Backstage, Gabriel and Camille pored over the scores, frantically searching for hidden keys and concealed harmonies. Each measure, each symbol, suddenly took on a mysterious meaning, as if the music itself had become the vehicle for an ancestral resistance. In the past, Éléonore had hidden a precious score in the folds of a stage dress, hoping to preserve the stifled voice of truth. The Count, ever hungry for control and power, slowly tightened his grip on those he suspected of being linked to the dissidents. The notes scribbled by Aurélien had become a threatening echo of a musical uprising, and his suspicions grew like a storm in his tormented mind.

Meanwhile, Gabriel found himself facing direct threats; his determination to uncover the secret of the scores became an increasingly perilous challenge. Every step in the deserted corridors of the Opera House seemed to echo like a warning. Still, his passion for the truth guided him inexorably toward the old, abandoned piano. He sensed that behind the worn keys lay the keystone of this story, buried in the centuries. As Gabriel's fingers touched the first notes, a shiver ran down his spine. The forgotten melodies seemed to whisper a call to action, to rebellion. Each trill, each modulation brought with it the vibrant breath of a tormented past, the promise of an imminent revelation. Rumours soon began to circulate around the Opera House, shrouding it in an aura of mystery that aroused both fascination and apprehension. Camille, Gabriel's faithful companion, shared his passion for the quest, deciphering with him the codes hidden at the heart of the buried compositions. The piano became a sacred vessel where the intertwined destinies of the past and present mingled, where the chords vibrated like oaths of rebellion and heroism. Thus, within the labyrinthine halls of the Opera House, seemingly insignificant notes gradually rose like banners of freedom, defying the heavy silence of oblivion. Music, once the silent accomplice of daring acts and clandestine struggles, resumed its role as the voice of rebellious souls, ready to shake the very foundations of buried history.

# 5
# The Masked Ball

Gabriel felt a rush of excitement as he stepped through the majestic doors of the Paris Opera House, masked as tradition dictates for a masked ball. At his side, Dr. CamilleFournier, looked stunning in her sparkling gown. The hall shimmered with dazzling lights, creating an enchanting atmosphere that permeated every corner of this cultural landmark. The guests, like ghosts from another time, moved gracefully through the grand theatre, hiding behind their masks, glances filled with curiosity and unspoken secrets.

Everything here was masks and mystery, a fateful setting conducive to disturbing revelations and unusual encounters. Sparkling jewels and sumptuous fabrics blended with the subtle scent of exquisite perfumes, enveloping everyone in a halo of mystery. In this hushed atmosphere, where confusing whispers and discreet laughter mingled, Gabriel and Camille blended into the crowd, like two shadows eager to thwart the workings of an ancient plot. They knew that this night would upset the established order and reveal secrets that had been buried for too long.

As they played their roles with subtlety, listening intently to the conversations that mingled in an unreal concert, an electric tension hung in the air, as if the whole of history were holding its breath to witness the dazzling resurgence of buried truths. The dancers' rhythmic footsteps seemed to punctuate the unfolding of their nocturnal investigation, drawing them ever deeper into a universe whose intricacies seemed unimaginable.

As the violins set the evening alight with their haunting melodies, Gabriel and Camille followed the invisible trail that would lead them to the very heart of the mysteries buried beneath the splendour of the Opera House. Time stood still in this bubble outside the world, belonging only to them, accomplices in a mission that united them beyond the boundaries of reality. As the hours passed, the plot unfolded, intertwining the destinies of characters from the past and present in an intoxicating whirlwind where fate itself seemed to play with masks and reveal its own face.

There they are, those sparkling masks dancing through the halls of the Opera, concealing identities and liberating tongues. Beneath this flamboyant finery lie souls in search of truth, spirits tormented by the secrets of the past. Every movement, every gesture becomes a riddle to be solved in this sumptuous setting, where history seems to repeat itself in a disturbing echo. In the midst of this feverish crowd, Éléonore bears the weight of a danger-ous role. Her mask hides much more than her face; it conceals the torments of a perilous mis-sion, the responsibility of preserving precious scores laden with coded messages. Her gaze sometimes wanders, fleeing beneath the glit-tering disguises, seeking to pierce the lies of this masked evening.

On the other side of the mirror, Gabriel and Camille are busy searching for traces of a buried past, tracking clues beneath the gild-ed decorations and lace veils. Their investiga-tion blends into the glittering ball, evolving like a spellbinding dance where each step brings them closer to the long-awaited revelation.

Meanwhile, the Count of Beaumont moves through the light, his haughty silhouette draw-ing all eyes to him. He gracefully displays his poisonous charm, seeking to steal more than a smile from the beautiful Éléonore. Beneath his false pretences, manipulation weaves its web, trapping hearts in a game of appearances that turns to tragedy. And while the dancers launch themselves into wild whirls, Raphaël slips away into the dark corridors, blinded by jealousy and manipulation that condemn him to betrayal. The setting exudes an atmosphere that is both enchanting and gloomy, blending the splen-dour of the finery with the ominous whispers of corrupt ambitions. Secret scores vibrate in harmony with the beating of hearts, infusing this worldly farandole with an underground rhythm. In this suspended moment, between two intertwined eras, destinies are shaped and shattered, truths are concealed and revealed, until the moment when the masks fall, revealing the heroic and treacherous faces that wrote history during this fateful night.


Masks adorned with feathers and jewels hid the faces of the guests. The Opera House sparkled with a thousand lights, like a star in the night sky. Gabriel watched each dancer, desperately searching for clues hidden behind their frozen smiles. Camille blended into the crowd, vigilant, ready to seize the slightest sign. The rustling of fabrics rivalled the intoxicating melodies emanating from the orchestra. The game of appearances had begun.

Amidst this dazzling parade, Éléonore moved with elusive grace. Her gaze locked with that of the Count of Beaumont, a pernicious glint of interest in her eyes. At her side, Aurélien hid his concern behind a polite smile, aware of the dangers that threatened their mission. The coded notes whispered in their ears, revealing the buried secrets of history. In the present, the frantic pace of Gabriel's footsteps contrasted with the languor of the waltzes of yesteryear.

The search for the hidden safe was turning into a personal quest, a nagging obsession. Every old portrait scrutinised, every corner explored was a struggle against oblivion, a struggle to preserve his heritage. The ancestral object in his hands vibrated with an indomitable aura, exhaling the heady scent of adventure.

As the evening unfolded, voices whispered convoluted rumours, pointing to each guest as a potential traitor. Raphaël, in the shadows, plotted his own schemes, blinded by passion and jealousy. His dilated pupils followed Éléonore's every move, feeding his growing resentment. Beneath the majestic chandeliers, destinies intertwined, weaving a complex web of lies and veiled truths. The two worlds, bound by centuries-old secrets, converged toward an imminent revelation, ready to unveil their mysteries. Between the glittering pomp and fragile alliances, the game of appearances was just beginning, precipitating its actors towards an inevitable dénouement.

The opera houses echoed with the haunting melodies of a forgotten past. At the same time, Gabriel and Camille delved into the twists and turns of a thousand-year-old intrigue. The musical scores concealed secrets, deciphering history through mysterious notes. Every turn in the corridor seemed to hum an ancient melody, enveloping the seekers in a bewitching and elusive aura. As they wandered through the masked hall, the dancing shadows seemed to whisper the forgotten story of the Desmoulins. Éléonore and Aurélien, like ghostly figures, had once tried to pierce the veil of ignorance, hiding their messages at the very heart of the musical compositions. The echoes of their historic struggles seemed to blend into the enchanting symphony that filled the Opera House, creating an invisible web between the glorious past and the uncertain present.

The challenge of unravelling these secret scores was immense for Gabriel and Camille. With each page turned, each note analysed, they came a little closer to the tenuous thread of their shared destiny with the Desmoulins. Their meticulous efforts were evidence of their burning desire to unravel the mystery, to understand the deep motivations that had led their ancestors to risk their lives to defend a just cause, hidden behind subtle musical variations.

Time seemed to stand still, as if the centuries had gathered at a masked ball of history to reveal its most intimate secrets. Each step on the dance floor echoed like an ancestral heartbeat, each mask concealing a face that could have belonged to a conspirator or an intrepid hero.

In this atmosphere of mystery and intrigue, the investigators' thoughts mingled with the whispers of the scores, creating a unique harmony between the search for truth and the fleeting beauty of art. The mission to decipher these secret scores was much more than a simple quest for knowledge: it was an attempt to plunge back into the very soul of a forgotten era, to rediscover the ideals buried beneath the layers of time. By unveiling the secrets embedded in these musical lines, Gabriel and Camille took part in a frantic ballet where each step brought them closer to a shocking revelation that could change the course of history while tinging their present lives with an aura of holy intensity.

The first notes of the orchestra filled the ballroom with an enchanting, spellbinding melody. The guests, draped in sumptuous attire and concealed behind elegant masks, danced gracefully, twirling lightly to the haunting rhythm of the music. The sparkling chandeliers cast golden reflections on the panelled walls, creating an almost supernatural, unreal atmosphere.

At the heart of this enchantment, the Count of Beaumont appeared like a majestic beast, his presence and charm arousing the envious admiration of the ladies and the jealousy of the gentlemen. His velvety gaze fell on Éléonore, dressed like a mysterious nymph. Their hands met in a spellbinding waltz, unleashing a whirlwind of confused and troubled feelings. As they danced, the Count deployed all his powers of seduction, using honeyed words to captivate Éléonore's attention. He whispered sweet nothings to her, stirring up a growing turmoil in the young woman's heart. As they whirled around, a wind of tension hung in the air, palpable in the inquisitive glances and hushed murmurs commenting on their unusual closeness.

Meanwhile, Gabriel and Camille navigated skillfully among the guests, closely observing every exchange, on the lookout for the slightest clue. Their masks concealed their true identities, propelling them into a subtle dance where shadow and light intermingled. They watched for the slightest gesture, the slightest inflexion of voice, aware that the balance of the evening could tip into intrigue and danger at any moment.

In this hushed atmosphere, Raphaël, consumed by jealousy, watched the couple with growing bitterness. Consumed by passionate madness, he was the unhappy spectator of a scene that brought his inner torments to the surface. His eyes, filled with unfulfilled desires, followed the Count and Éléonore's every step, revealing a latent animosity ready to erupt.

Thus, at the heart of these two masked balls, games of illusion and seduction were unfolding, intertwining past and present destinies. The plot thickened inexorably around these tormented souls, promising explosive revelations and conspiracies that were just waiting to come to light.


The Opera House was full of mystery that evening. As the Count of Beaumont danced elegantly with Éléonore, a palpable tension hung in the air. In a dark corner, Raphaël watched the scene with eyes filled with jealousy. His silhouette blended into the shadows, but his inner turmoil overshadowed any attempt at discretion.

For several weeks, the Count's presence alongside Éléonore had plunged Raphaël into an abyss of torment. The young woman, whose dazzling beauty, shrouded in mystery, continued to charm the ball's guests, seemed captivated by the nobleman's presence. The masked ball offered everyone the opportunity to lose themselves in an illusion of freedom.

Still, for Raphaël, it crystallised the invisible chains of his unrequited passion. As laughter and music filled the room, a dark revelation emerged in Raphaël's mind: did the Count know of Éléonore's true intentions within the clandestine circle? The growing closeness between them fueled the flames of suspicion within him. The carefree ballet of the dancers became a reflection of his inner turmoil, torn between desire and mistrust. Unable to hide his distress any longer, Raphaël sought refuge in the darkness of a secluded corner. His gaze, haunted by grief, wandered over the golden frescoes that adorned the walls of the Opera House. Muffled voices mingled with the music, plunging Raphaël further into an abyss of doubt and resignation. At the heart of this pulsating ball, Raphaël's bitterness crystallised the intrigue that enveloped all the masked guests. Shadows danced in a tormented symphony, reflecting the unspoken passions that shimmered within the Opera House. And in the midst of this turmoil, a revelation was about to burst forth, plunging the masked assembly into the disturbing chiaroscuro of betrayal and revenge.

As the violins resonate, the halls of the Opera sparkle under the light of the glittering chandeliers. Masked faces cross paths, whirling in a mesmerising ballet, concealing secrets and desires. At the heart of this worldly whirlwind, Éléonore, dressed in her sumptuous, bright blue gown, exudes an aura of mystery that attracts attention. At the side of the Comte de

Beaumont, her clay mask sculpted with refinement, she appears radiant. Still, a glimmer of worry flashes across her azure eyes from time to time.

Meanwhile, behind the scenes at the Opera House, Gabriel and Camille explore the dark labyrinth, searching for the slightest trace of the past. By the flickering light of their torch, shadows dance on the walls, revealing an eerie atmosphere steeped in mystery. Suddenly, a soft click sounds, heralding a crucial discovery. A chest buried for decades lies there, a silent witness to past events. Gabriel slowly traces the arabesques adorning the latch, frozen in time with his fingertips.

At the same time, the muffled echo of distant waltzes fills the air. Nervously, they open the chest, revealing buried treasures, documents yellowed by time, sheet music with faded notes, and coded correspondence. Among them, one object immediately catches Gabriel's attention: a silver brooch adorned with enigmatic symbols that he recognises instantly. In the impenetrable darkness, a light seems to shine through, casting a new light on Gabriel's meticulous quest.

Meanwhile, at the ball, the atmosphere grows heavy, as if weighed down by the secret. Beneath her graceful mask, Éléonore feels a growing anxiety rising within her. The Count of Beaumont, like a predator on the prowl, continues his feigned gallantries, using his charm to try to win the young woman's trust. But already, the invisible threads of betrayal are tightening around them, threatening to engulf everything in a dangerous abyss.

As the hours pass, the intertwined destinies of Gabriel and Éléonore seem to converge toward an inevitable climax. In this tumultuous dance between lies and truths, each step taken reveals the shadow of history, ready to unfold in all its dark splendour. The masks, symbols of a distorted reality, hide much more than just faces: they conceal the intricacies of a complex web, where secrets and manipulation weave a deadly melody. And while Gabriel contemplates the inherited brooch, Éléonore, trapped by social conventions, discovers that the clarity hidden in darkness can bring its share of poignant revelations.

In the intoxicating atmosphere of the masked ball at the Opera, Gabriel and Camille slipped away from prying eyes to explore the room where one of Gabriel's ancestors had hidden his secrets for decades. The flickering candlelight cast dancing shadows on the walls. At the same time, the muffled murmurs of music floated in the air, heavy with mystery. As they moved forward, a golden glow revealed itself, emanating from a forgotten corner of the room. It was the chest mentioned in the family chronicles, containing the long-awaited answers. The metal was weathered by time, adorned with ancient symbols that seemed to come to life in the candlelight.

Upon opening it, Gabriel discovered a fan of yellowed parchments and delicately rolled letters, testifying to his ancestor's passion and commitment. Among these dusty treasures, one object immediately caught his eye: a pendant adorned with a chiselled medallion, once worn by Aurélien Desmoulins himself. The shine of the silver contrasted with the striking similarity between the face engraved on the medallion and Gabriel's own. It was then that a feeling of deep connection with the past came over him, as if ancient voices were whispering in his ears, inviting him to pierce the veil of time.

Camille, meanwhile, couldn't help but be captivated by a series of sheet music carefully hidden at the bottom of the chest. These coded melodies seemed to seal a secret pact between the ages, each skillfully weaving together the threads of destiny. Slowly, she began to decipher them, bringing out the beauty and truth of the intertwined notes, revealing the musical mysteries of the past.

As the night wore on and the masked ball

continued to enchant the guests, Gabriel and Camille immersed themselves in the treasures of the past, illuminating forgotten chapters of family history and unveiling long-held secrets. Each document, each relic exuded ancient scents, whispering forgotten stories and buried truths. In this intimacy veiled by heritage, they rediscovered the thread of a hidden story, their souls vibrating to the rhythm of discoveries that brought them inexorably closer to their shared destiny.

The chest, like a remnant of a misty past, slowly emerged from the dusty floor. Its worn contours told the unique story of a bygone era, whose mysteries had not yet revealed all their secrets. Gabriel approached cautiously, as if afraid of disturbing the fragile balance between the past and the present. The unknown ancestor who had once owned this precious artefact seemed to guide his steps, giving him a mission that went beyond his simple quest for truth.

Opening the chest with almost religious solemnity, he discovered a beautifully crafted object that seemed to pulsate with long-buried energy. A symbol-laden amulet, enigmatic yet familiar, seemed to link past and present in an indissoluble tangle. Camille watched, fascinated by the revelation of this ancestral legacy, sensing that their destinies were now intimately intertwined with those of the protagonists of the past. The detailed engravings on the amulet seemed to whisper coded messages from another time, calling Gabriel to continue the quest begun by his ancestor. A halo of golden light radiated from the confined space of the tunnel, as if to signal that the legacy left behind could no longer be ignored. With the chest closed and the amulet carefully wrapped, Gabriel felt a new determination rise within him, mixed with a sense of humility in the face of this ancestral burden. Together, they knew that this relic would seal their destiny forever.

Gabriel felt the icy grip of doubt envelop him as his fingers brushed against the ancient relics, silent witnesses to the tortuous paths of history. The object, once prized by his ancestor Aurélien, now revealed secrets buried in the shadows of centuries. Sitting in front of the chest stolen over time, Gabriel and Camille embarked on a captivating exploration, plunging into the heart of a mystery steeped in betrayal and revenge. With their eyes fixed on the tattered parchment, the pair pieced together a complex web of hidden truths and carefully woven lies. Each object recovered, each word deciphered, shed a dark light on the murky twists and turns of the past. Between the yellowed and dog-eared pages of Aurélien's diaries, the bitter image of an unsuspected betrayal began to emerge.

His breath stifled by overwhelming emotion, Gabriel plunged into the memories of the past, confronted with a tormented abyss where loyalty and disloyalty intertwined. In a ballet of chilling revelations, the traitorous figure emerged, whose name, engraved in the hidden archives, shed new light on the unspeakable perfidy. Each stroke, each wicked imprint opened a gaping breach into the conspiracy hatched long ago and the gaping scars it left behind. A spell cast by a turbulent past, the betrayal woven into the fabric of time arrogantly defied the fine line between loyalty and deceit.

Amidst enigmatic phrases, the growing shadow of a treacherous sentinel materialised, shaking the foundations of trust. Cryptic tales and heart-rending farewells all contributed to this grim picture, guided by the imperious hand of concealment and confusion. As Gabriel skillfully untangled the deceptive web, his pupils reflected the bitter disillusionment that was taking root in the intertwined lines.

As the hours passed in the relentless quest for forgotten truths, the faces of the past came to life, punctuating the fatal ballet of dead illusions. In this sanctuary of repressed knowledge, the final piece of the puzzle, still exhaling the heady scent of conspiracy, came to light, tearing away the purple veil draped over the tragedy of the past. Thus, with his scrutinising eye fixed on the ancestral betrayal, Gabriel understood that from these buried mistakes arose the priceless seeds of redemption and deliverance.

# 6

# The Betrayal Revealed

In the narrow darkness of the secret room, the metallic creaking of the safe mechanism echoed in the confined space. Gabriel and Camille were immersed in intense silence, their minds focused on deciphering the thousand-year-old riddle. Gabriel's nimble fingers carefully manipulated the ancient dials.

At the same time, Camille, armed with her encyclopedic knowledge, illuminated each gesture with her erudition. Every click, every tremor of the lock seemed to reveal a new facet of the clandestine history that had been sealed away over the centuries. Time seemed to stand still, their breath held in feverish anticipation of an imminent discovery.

Suddenly, a dull click filled the room, and the safe finally released its hidden mysteries. Inside, parchments yellowed by time seemed to burn with an invisible light, silent witnesses to events long past. Gabriel's trembling fingers grasped these treasures from another age, tenderly unfolding each sheet laden with stories and secrets. Camille approached, illuminating the ancient writings with her oil lamp, revealing cryptic inscriptions and enigmatic drawings.

Before their astonished eyes, the engraved symbols told of forgotten legends, political plots, and unspoken betrayals. In the folds of the parchment, history shone in all its grandeur and complexity, opening a window onto a world swallowed up by the shadows of the past.

The hours passed without them noticing, absorbed by the infinite richness of these ancient treasures. Each word, each illustration, transported Gabriel and Camille to a distant universe where every dream fueled the flame of intrigue and adventure. No stone was left unturned in the very fabric of their reality. Each secret uncovered was a fragile link woven between yesterday and today, a fragrant bridge spanning the ages to lead them to truth and fulfilment. Thus, in that precious moment, the heroic historian and the wise scholar knew that their destinies had been bound together in that instant, that every effort, every sacrifice, had reached its apotheosis in the flickering glow of the ancient parchments. And as the outside world continued to turn, they remained motionless, captivated by this fleeting embrace that connected them to a past seven thousand years old and to their mission, carried out with virtuosity.

Their hearts still filled with emotion at their unexpected discovery, Gabriel and Camille gazed with a mixture of apprehension and curiosity at the precious parchments revealed by the opening of the chest, as if they contained within them the weight of centuries past. With trembling fingers, Gabriel touched the ancient characters engraved on the centuries-old paper.

At the same time, Camille, seized by the importance of the moment, held her breath. The words of the past seemed to come to life before their eyes, revealing the secrets of a troubled era and the undeniable links between the people of the past and their contemporary destinies. The ancient writing evoked the torments of a broken family, the plots hatched in the shadows, and the thwarted loves that had marked the fate of Gabriel's ancestors. Each line traced resonated like an echo from the past, an indelible mark passed down through the ages, arousing in the two researchers a deep empathy for the forgotten figures of this family saga. As they pored over these stories stolen from time, an unrelenting truth emerged before their astonished eyes, revealing the complex web of intertwined destinies. The hushed rumours, the hidden conspiracies, everything took shape in the flickering light of truth, illuminating the grey areas that had marked the history of the Desmoulins family.

The parchments gave a voice to the forgotten, conferring a moving legitimacy on the sacrifices made by their ancestors, like poignant testimonies on which Gabriel's entire legacy rested. As the revelations piled up, an oppressive tension filled the room, the silence becoming an accomplice to the intimate revelations whispered by the worn-out writings. The fate of the Desmoulins family was sealed in these pages, bearing a tragedy that had been buried for too long under the veneer of a biased history. Justice refused to hide its missteps any longer.

The trials of this distant past became the catalyst for a unique quest, calling Gabriel and Camille to reconstruct the family puzzle, piece by piece, to restore the balance broken by treachery and darkness. Thus, the parchments that had remained silent for so many years now revealed their secrets, illuminating the tortuous path taken by Gabriel's ancestors and confirming the unbreakable bond that united the generations through an ancestral struggle. The two researchers were now entrusted with a crucial mission: to unravel the mysteries lost in the mists of time, to restore the honour that had been trampled upon, and to exalt the memory of a tormented legacy.

As the noose tightened around Gabriel and Camille, an unexpected event disrupted their quest for the truth. In the darkness of the room where they were studying the revelations of the precious parchments, a figure suddenly appeared, shattering the heavy silence that reigned. It was the heir, whose menacing presence seemed to haunt every corner of the Desmoulins' destiny. His gaze, filled with determination and greed, challenged the two researchers, frozen in time. The descendant of Beaumont had insinuated himself like a vengeful spectre into the very heart of their quest for truth.

An electric tension filled the air, revealing how much this encounter would seal the fate that hung in the balance. Gabriel, driven by a burning passion, immediately understood the crucial importance of this silent confrontation. As his fingers brushed against the relics of the past, he felt a fierce determination rise within him to protect the memory of his ancestors. Camille, his faithful companion in misfortune and vigilant guardian of the hidden knowledge, displayed an indomitable resolve, as if she were ready to face any danger to preserve what had been revealed.

The heir, impenetrable and hieratic, gave nothing away, hiding his dark intentions behind his haughty demeanour. Time seemed to stand still, frozen in feverish anticipation of the events to come. The damning documents lay in Gabriel's trembling hands, while the heir's menacing shadow loomed like an imminent threat. The stakes of this confrontation went far beyond personal ambitions. It was an ancestral struggle taking shape, intertwining the complex threads of the past and present in a timeless clash. Secrets buried for decades were suddenly unearthed, ready to shed light on the truth suppressed by the intrigues and betrayals of another time. In Gabriel's eyes, a spark of defiance burned brightly, witness to his fierce determination not to give in to adversity. Camille, a symbol of quiet strength, embodied with unwavering dignity the stubborn resistance against the torments that stood in their way. And the heir, the unchanging guardian of dark family secrets, held in his eager hands the uncertain future of all these intertwined lives. The struggle for truth was only just beginning, and each was preparing to fight to the last breath to defend their convictions. In the smoky depths of history, the appearance of the heir signalled the beginning of an epic struggle that would determine the fate of entire generations grappling with a legacy as glorious as it was perilous.

The intensity of the revelation weighed heavily on Gabriel and Camille's shoulders. They knew that every second counted, that the slightest mistake could seal their fate forever.

As they delved into the depths of these damning documents, an aura of determination filled the dark room where past and present mingled dangerously. Every word, every symbol, every line drawn on these ancient parchments painted a dark picture in which the unspeakable truth was hidden. The stakes were much higher than they had imagined. Beaumont's descendant was a menacing shadow, ready to do anything to hide the secrets of his lineage. In the past, betrayal had been revealed within the circle, triggering an avalanche of lies and treacherous manoeuvres. The Count, armed with ruthless authority, had ordered the arrest of all members of the group, condemning innocent souls to a dark and freezing night in the City's dungeons.

Meanwhile, Éléonore and Raphaël, wandering through the winding tunnels, desperately sought refuge, fleeing a fate already sealed by their courageous commitment. In this frantic race for the truth, Gabriel and Camille came face to face with the terrifying darkness of corrupt power. Each line traced on the yellowed petals of the past echoed like a whisper from lost souls, guiding them inexorably toward the resolution of a treacherous mystery. In their struggle to uncover the truth, they had to face their deepest fears, braving the adversity of a descendant determined to protect his family's cursed legacy.

The oppressive tension became palpable, each breath a discordant note in a sinister symphony. Despite the seemingly insurmountable trials, the echoes of past actions converged with the determination of the present. The struggle for truth was reflected in every glance, every gesture, every sigh. Gabriel and Camille found themselves at the heart of a battle whose stakes far exceeded their own history. It was a struggle for justice, a fight to honour those who had sacrificed their freedom for a nobler ideal. And in this merciless struggle, the flickering hope of victory continued to burn, like a beacon in the tormented darkness of humanity.

The members of the secret circle were gathered in the hidden library, lit by the faint glow of candles. An atmosphere of mystery and apprehension hung in the air as everyone pored over the recently discovered parchments. Faces were tense, eyes darting around the room. Aurélien, usually so confident, seemed deeply troubled. Gabriel, accompanied by Camille, studied the documents unearthed from the safe with feverish attention. Ancient writings revealed unimaginable secrets. The words inscribed on the old parchment seemed to leap out like bolts of lightning, shattering old certainties and giving way to brutal truth. As the tension mounted, a dark figure suddenly appeared in the doorway.

Beaumont's descendant, his face contorted with greed, burst into the room, sucking all the oxygen out of it. His greedy gaze swept over the precious documents and then froze on Gabriel, sparkling with fierce hatred. A heavy silence fell, broken only by the crackling of the candles. The revelation of treachery within the circle could no longer be ignored. Everyone now realised that there was a traitor among them, willing to do anything to serve his own interests. The trust that had long existed between the members was shattered. Whispers and accusing glances filled the room. Alliances dissolved, replaced by palpable mistrust.

Meanwhile, in the past, the Count of Beaumont secretly passed a decree to his henchmen, ordering the immediate arrest of all members of the circle. Chaos reigned as the forces of law and order stormed the secret library, brutally ending the circle members' hopes of freedom and revolution. Éléonore and Raphaël, caught in this ruthless plot, realised they had to seek refuge in the dark depths of the underground tunnel. Their footsteps echoed through the winding passages as they fought to preserve their freedom, their very lives. The betrayal had borne its deadly fruit, plunging the clandestine circle into unprecedented turmoil.

The day of glory was about to give way to darkness. The Count, enraged by the betrayal within his inner circle, issued a sinister decree that would seal the fate of the transgressors. His dark figure paced the ancestral mansion, his cloak floating like a cursed spectre. The corridors echoed with his heavy footsteps, like a sinister symphony announcing the punishment to come. The ancient parchments were silent in the face of the Count's immeasurable anger. Still, his fiery, piercing eyes burned every line of betrayed loyalty. The flames of the candle danced uneasily, captive to the Count's inner storm.

Suddenly, overcome by uncontrollable fury, he brandished the decree before his loyal servants. At the same time, the glow of the brazier revealed the bold strokes of the draconian writing. Imposing silence and terror, the decree ordered the immediate arrest of all members accused of conspiracy against his honour and that of the noble Beaumont lineage. The sentence was crystal clear, without appeal or mercy: life imprisonment in the cold, damp dungeons of the manor. No leniency would be shown, no repentance would soften the sentence. The air suddenly became charged with oppressive electricity as the decree fell like the axe of secular justice. The muffled whispers and furtive glances were evidence of the impending explosion. Factions formed, alliances broke, and the black shadow of betrayal enveloped the ancestral manor of Beaumont.

Meanwhile, uncertainty gripped Éléonore and Raphaël, forced to flee to escape the Count's relentless wrath. In the frightening darkness of the Paris underground, they would have to face their own demons and their own choices to hope for a future that defied their inevitable downfall. And above them, the threatening echoes of the decree resounded in their exile, condemning them forever to the icy breath of betrayal.

The calm of the Paris underground is the silent backdrop to Éléonore and Raphaël's escape. Their short breaths and racing hearts set the pace for their frantic race to an uncertain refuge. In the oppressive darkness of the tunnel, where only the murmur of their footsteps breaks the silence, they desperately seek shelter from the relentless pursuit of the Count of Beaumont. The menacing shadows, combined with the haunting echoes of their pursuers, remind the two fugitives of the magnitude of their peril.

Éléonore, the embodiment of feminine determination, guides Raphaël through the underground labyrinth with a confidence worthy of the heroines of ancient tragedies. Despite her youth, she is fearless, ready to do anything to preserve the clandestine legacy of her brother and herself.

However, the darkness also reveals the cracks that are creeping into their mutual trust. The distraught looks they exchange betray a growing anxiety, inexorably fueled by every sinister echo coming from behind or ahead, a sign of the inevitable ambush that awaits them. The icy feel of the damp ground beneath their bare feet, the musky scent of forgotten passageways haunted by ghosts of the past, all combine to plunge our two fugitives into an almost surreal trance. Each heartbeat seems to sound the death knell of a freedom already doomed.

At the same time, the indistinct line between hope and despair materialises in the suffocating darkness. And yet, beyond the weariness that weighs heavily on their limbs, each step becomes a symbol of their relentless struggle for survival. For in this hellish labyrinth, imbued with the acrid smell of passing time and the ink of unspoken secrets, they carry with them not only the memory of unjustly banished patriots but also the fragile sparkle of a cherished ideal, the cornerstone of their quest.

Thus, in the agony of their flight, as the flickering light of a distant exit teases their hopes, Éléonore and Raphaël transcend their fear and draw from deep within themselves an unsuspected strength, fueled by the fertile memory of fallen heroes and legends yet to be written. Their hurried, steady footsteps, though betraying the urgency of their vital escape, sum up the fierce determination that dwells in their trembling souls. And as the walls ooze their intangible and enigmatic secrets, our fugitives press on, carrying a hope that nothing and no one can take away.

As betrayal suddenly reared its ugly head within the clandestine circle, Éléonore and Raphaël were forced to seek refuge in the labyrinthine underground tunnels of Paris. The flickering light of a candle revealed an uncertain future. Still, they knew they must remain hopeful despite the oppression weighing heavily on their shoulders. The damp walls seemed to whisper ancient stories, half-erased by the passing centuries. As they moved forward, the haunting clatter of their heels echoed, amplified by the oppressive silence of the place. Each echo seemed to point to the past and resonate in the present, reminding the fugitives of their quest for justice. Fear only made them more determined to safeguard the secrets hidden beneath the cobblestones of the City of Light. Suddenly, a shadow loomed before them, cast by a dark cavity nestled in the crook of a tunnel.

Éléonore held her breath, unsure of the origin of this menacing figure. The seconds stretched into hours in the tormented darkness, until Raphaël recognised a familiar face. It was the guardian of the place, a loyal companion of the circle for years, whose loyalty was undeniable. He led them to a secret sanctuary hidden in the bowels of Paris, a place where hope could flourish, safe from prying eyes.

There, huddled around a modest fire, Éléonore and Raphaël shared their fears, but also their dreams of freedom. The flickering flame danced on the damp walls, casting fleeting reflections that seemed to whisper promises of a better future. In this unexpected refuge, illuminated by forbidden knowledge, they were faced with a dilemma of trust: should they share these crucial discoveries with an outside ally, at the risk of compromising their safety?

Yet, each knew that to triumph, they would need the support of courageous souls, ready to defend the truth against the greed of the established power structures. As the days passed in this hidden lair, Éléonore and Raphaël forged an alliance worthy of eternity. Their minds were nourished by the writings and teachings of those who had fought before them for justice and enlightenment. The desire to restore the honour of the unjustly condemned grew within them, galvanising their hearts wounded by betrayal. Every moment spent in those dark vaults strengthened their resolve, bringing them closer to a conclusion where truth would triumph over the malicious schemes of those who had made a pact with greed and lies. But the menacing shadow of the Count of Beaumont still hung over them, forcing them to act with caution and discernment, for the future of all rested in their hands.

The damning documents discovered by Gabriel and Camille plunged them into an abyss of doubt. The evidence revealed long-buried secrets, casting a sinister light on once-revered figures. Faced with this ruthless truth, the very essence of their faith in their family legacy was shaken. As Beaumont's descendant emerged with the firm intention of seizing the precious revelations, a palpable tension filled the room. The two researchers were faced with a crucial choice: hand over the evidence to the authorities or conceal it to protect their reputations and the fragile peace in which they had lived until then. The weight of their decision crystallised centuries of honour and tradition, but also their intrinsic trust in those who had come before them.

Meanwhile, in the depths of the past, within the clandestine circle, the veil of betrayal was torn apart. Looks turned to suspicion, allegiances were questioned, and a shadow of mistrust hung over every word spoken. The Count of Beaumont, driven by pride and anger, ordered the merciless arrest of all his former companions. In the rush, Éléonore and Raphaël were forced to flee into the saving darkness of the tunnel, where their laboured breathing mingled with the silence of the ancient stone. Back in the present, the echo of Beaumont's descendant's footsteps resounded through the room, testing Gabriel and Camille's resolve. Grappling with the troubling legacy that had been revealed to them, they faced the most critical moment of their quest. The tension mounted as each hesitated between loyalty to family history and disillusionment in the face of an unsuspected reality. The stakes went beyond the fate of a few individuals; they threatened to compromise the legitimacy of an entire lineage, savagely shaken by the irreversible impact of the secrets that had been revealed.


Ever since Gabriel and Camille had got their

hands on the compromising documents hidden in the mysterious safe, a palpable tension had hung in the air. The parchments revealed secrets that shook the very foundations of the Paris Opera, casting a sinister light on occult machinations and unimaginable betrayals.

For days, the two accomplices had studied the ancient writings with meticulous attention, piecing together the pieces of a diabolical puzzle. Every word, every symbol seemed to hold mystical power, as if they were silent witnesses to a long-forgotten history. It was in this state of frantic investigation that Beaumont's descendant appeared, like a spectre come to claim his share of a cursed inheritance. His presence was the embodiment of menace, a cruel reminder that the past could rise up to haunt the present. He scrutinised Gabriel and Camille's discoveries with boundless greed, determined to erase any incriminating evidence. An inevitable confrontation was brewing between the zealous guardian of family secrets and the defenders of truth.

Meanwhile, in the bowels of the Opera House, the story of the past continued in equally dramatic fashion. The Count, hungry for revenge, had launched a merciless hunt for the members of the clandestine circle. Arrests rained down like a devastating storm, sweeping away the hopes and dreams of those who dared to defy the established order.

Éléonore and Raphaël, surrounded by the shadows of betrayal, found refuge in the forgotten corners of an ancient tunnel, ready to do anything to escape their grim fate. Thus, destiny intertwined the threads of the past and the present, weaving a complex web where each revelation fueled the suspense.

Each discovery made by Gabriel and Camille echoed in the depths of the old theatre, resonating like the desperate cries of those who had been crushed by the relentless wheels of history. Face to face with the past, the future seemed suspended in unbearable tension, a crucial moment when modern heroes had to confront the ghosts of their ancestors to pierce the darkness and restore the honour of the fallen.

# 7
# The Race Against Time

Gabriel and Camille's hurried footsteps echoed through the winding alleys of the old town, accompanied by the frantic beating of their hearts. The shadows of the night closed in around them, seeming to block their escape. In this labyrinth of darkness, each street embraced its procession of ancient mysteries, exhaling the tormented soul of centuries past. Pursued under the silvery moon, the two accomplices frantically sought refuge and answers to the nagging questions that haunted their minds. The whispers of the past seemed to mingle with the breath of the wind, blurring the boundaries between the present and history. In ancient times, Aurélien, Éléonore, and Raphaël had shared this same desperate flight, hunted like fugitives in the underground labyrinth of Paris.

The agonising embrace of danger seemed to weave an invisible bond between the eras, intertwining destinies with relentless ferocity. As the turmoil in the alleys seemed to conceal a troubled past and an imminent threat, Gabriel and Camille sensed that their disturbing discoveries had awakened evil forces, ready to do anything to preserve their dark secret. Each document they analysed only served to fan the embers of a forgotten financial scandal, transforming the yellowed parchments into silent witnesses to an unbearable truth. In the ghostly moonlight, they could make out the menacing silhouette of an invisible enemy, orchestrating their hunt with cruelty skilfully concealed in the shadows. The echoes of the past seemed to resonate with every step, reminding them that nothing was ever truly buried in the depths of history. As fear radiated from the deserted alleys, a fierce determination suddenly animated Gabriel's gaze.

Aurélien's insight seemed to inhabit his every movement, infusing his actions with an unexpected heroism. The hours spent deciphering obscure codes seemed to take on new meaning in this race against time, where truth was the only light to follow. They knew the night would be long, strewn with pitfalls and traps set by an elusive hand. Yet, the determined gleam in their eyes reflected a silent promise not to falter in the face of adversity, to pursue their desperate quest for justice at all costs. For on this night, when everything was hanging in the balance, a mere glimmer of hope could illuminate the surrounding darkness, transforming the hunt into an epic quest to restore the truth and the honour of their ancestors.


The dark maze of underground corridors seemed to close in on Gabriel and Camille as they rushed into the oppressive darkness. Their footsteps echoed like the rapid beating of a frantic heart, their laboured breathing betraying the terror that gripped them. The flames of the torches flickered, casting shifting shadows on the damp walls, turning every corner into a potential trap.

In their desperate race, Gabriel's thoughts drifted between past and present, between the mysteries of the 19th Century and the present dangers threatening their lives. Was it fate that had led them into these underground depths, or was it a more sinister force, plotting its dark designs for centuries?

Suddenly, a distant rumbling echoed through the labyrinth, amplifying their anguish. The threat loomed, like an intangible but oppressive spectre, ready to materialise in every dark corner. Each step became a struggle against oblivion, a test to preserve their breath as night engulfed their fleeting silhouettes. In the suffocating darkness, their presence seemed insignificant, drowned in the bowels of the earth, like a lost note in a chaotic symphony.

The memory of the 19th-century protagonists, pursued through the same ancient vaults, crossed Gabriel's mind. Aurélien, Éléonore, and Raphaël, once confronted with the same relentless hunt orchestrated by the Count of Beaumont, seemed to share this grim fate with them. The echoes of the past seemed to vibrate between the stone walls, bearing unspeakable secrets and treacherous conspiracies, silent witnesses to past struggles.

As the darkness threatened to engulf them, a glimmer of hope emerged in Gabriel's mind. He remembered the documents they had discovered, those precious pieces of the ancient puzzle, and a flash of clarity illuminated his gaze. If they could decipher the code hidden in those pages yellowed by time, perhaps they would find the key to thwart the age-old plot that surrounded them. A fierce determination then fuelled their escape, like an offering to the dawning clarity that would seal their salvation. For under the pale moon, they were determined to defy the shadows that pursued them, to exalt their courage in the face of relentless darkness.


Footsteps echo in the dark, damp corridors, where every shadow seems to conceal a thousand-year-old mystery. The flickering flames of the torches highlight the forgotten architecture, revealing ancient frescoes and mysterious engravings. Gabriel and Camille advance cautiously, their footsteps echoing like a sound from centuries past. Beneath the stone vault, the whispers of the past seem to grow louder, evoking secrets buried for too long.

The torchlight casts shifting silhouettes, cutting the walls with its fleeting presence. Every corner seems to hold a hidden treasure, an elusive truth that plays with the intrepid explorers. An aura of antiquity hangs in the air, mingled with a palpable sense of danger. Light breezes carry distant echoes and indistinct whispers, as if the walls themselves were murmuring forgotten stories. The plot thickens in the dark labyrinth, as the present collides with the vestiges of a troubled past.

With handwritten documents in hand, Gabriel and Camille attempt to decipher the clues hidden in the ancient texts. Each parchment contains a piece of the truth, but also a potential trap. Words intertwine in a disturbing ballet, painting a picture of a financial conspiracy linked to the 19th Century. As the torchlight flickers, suspicions grow and merge with the threats of the present. Reality and history intertwine in a macabre dance, fighting a merciless battle against the shadow of conspiracy that hangs over these venerable walls. In this labyrinth of forgotten knowledge, each step echoes like a challenge to the darkness that seeks to conceal the truth. Between the ghosts of the past and the threats of the present, Gabriel and Camille continue their quest, determined to break the centuries-old silence and reveal the hidden face of history.

As torchlight flickers in the winding corridors, Gabriel and Camille find themselves trapped in a maze of ancient secrets. The spectres of the past seem to whisper through the stone walls, evoking unspeakable plots and doomed destinies. Every creak of the floorboards echoes like a warning, reminding the intrepid seekers that danger lurks around every corner.

Meanwhile, in a Paris plunged into darkness, Beaumont's descendant plots with cold determination. His merciless gaze betrays his sinister intentions, and he seems willing to do anything to keep the secrets buried in the limbo of time. Like a vengeful shadow, he casts his threat over the innocent Camille, endangering not only her life but also the long-hidden truth. As the protagonists of the 19th Century face their own pursuit beneath the cobblestones of the City of Light, fate seems to push them to relive ancestral torments, as if the past and the present were. Still, an echo mingled with intrigue and inextricable dangers. The yellowed pages of ancient documents gradually unearth the ramifications of a financial scandal of unsuspected magnitude, giving this cursed legacy a demonic aura. From all this, Gabriel senses the blaze of a thousand-year-old inferno, striving to piece together the scattered pieces of the infernal plot. Passing through forgotten crypts and brushing against buried mysteries, he advances like a phoenix engulfed in the flames of passion and discovery. In the midst of the darkness, the hope of unearthing the truth persists, like a fragile torch guiding the steps of valiant hearts, ready to face the darkness to restore the splendour of justice.

The tension was palpable in the confined atmosphere of the underground passages, where time seemed to stand still, tinged with oppressive anxiety. Gabriel and Camille pressed themselves against the cold walls, their ragged breathing echoing in the darkness. Each moment felt like an eternity as they continued their breathless race through the stone labyrinth that whispered echoes of buried secrets. In this underground maze, the yellowed parchments exhaled a scent of dust and mystery. As their hands trembled, handling them with care, the cryptic words seemed to quiver beneath their fingertips. Each ancient word concealed an unexplored universe, a tortuous past lurking in the shadows, waiting to be revealed.

The sound of their footsteps echoed like a heartbeat in this ancient enclosure, carrying the whispers of centuries past. Each line traced by a distant pen seemed to shiver with an urgent need to be heard, deciphered, understood. The voices of the past seemed to rise slowly from the yellowed pages, as if to narrate scattered events, weave the threads of destiny, and reveal the lies intertwined over time.

The flickering candlelight cast dancing shadows on the writings preserved in the forgotten corners of this underground world. Each word, each symbol, each drawing came to life in the flickering glow, vibrating with its own story, offering history-hungry researchers a glimpse of the hidden truth. Ancient knowledge seemed to whisper in their ears, revealing unsuspected truths and plots hatched far from prying eyes. Hearts beat in unison with the gears of time, as revelations redrew history and shed light on areas that had been shrouded in darkness for too long. Each discovery shed light on a previously unknown part of existence, erasing the boundaries between eras, uniting the past and the present in a spellbinding dance, revealing a buried legacy and hinting at a future to be built on the shaky foundations of the past.

In this race against time, Gabriel and Camille find themselves immersed in a sea of ancient documents. Each parchment seems to contain the whispers of history, a history that strains through the lines of time to finally find its echo in the present. The yellowed pages unearth buried secrets, and each truth exposes centuries-old lies. Their quest becomes an uncertain dance between dusty libraries and mysterious cellars. They decipher coded correspondence, trace hidden financial flows, and a pattern of greed and betrayal gradually emerges before their astonished eyes. Each discovery brings them closer to the truth, but also to insidious danger. Huddled in these dark corners, Aurélien, Éléonore, and Raphaël seem to relive their desperate escape through the underground passages of the City of Light. A deadly pursuit propels them into a reality marked by terror and shadow.

The Count, the embodiment of menace and ferocity, watches them with icy determination. Their footsteps echo in the tunnels like a funeral march, and their breathing matches the oppressive tempo of urgency and oppression. The shadows stretching across the walls seem to whisper silent warnings, almost vertiginous imprecations.

The flickering candlelight reveals the fresh ink of the cursed writings, while Beaumont's descendant schemes slyly in the darkness of the present. His shadow looms menacingly over the fate of our protagonists, turning their quest into a fight to the death against a relentless enemy. Gabriel and Camille, caught between enigmas and peril, carve their names into the tumultuous epic of the centuries. Their minds ablaze with a thirst for authenticity, they open the locked doors of the past to release the fragments of hidden truth. Each symbol deciphered, each mystery solved, testifies to their unwavering determination to unravel the twists and turns of the plot. And in this frantic pursuit, fate seems to be pulling invisible strings to weave a web of intrigue and danger where the beings of yesterday and today intertwine in a hellish choreography.

The flickering torchlight cast erratic shadows on the damp stone walls as Gabriel and Camille ventured deeper and deeper into the secret bowels of the City. Each step echoed ominously in the mysterious tunnels, silent witnesses to so many buried stories. Sweat beaded on the foreheads of the two companions, their imminent capture weighing heavily on their shoulders. The urgency to find the key to unravel the web of mysteries that trapped them in a macabre dance between the past and the present was pressing.

The grey walls were punctuated by clues they feverishly unearthed, like a morbid treasure hunt. The memories of Aurélien, Éléonore, and Raphaël seemed to breathe through each relic they dug up. The dust of centuries past hung heavy in the air, creating an almost supernatural atmosphere that lent even the smallest objects an aura of sinister prophecy. Their fingers ran over the yellowed documents, deciphering words written by pens long since swallowed by time, releasing the light of hidden revelations.

Yet, the menacing shadow of Beaumont's descendant loomed insidiously over their struggle. Like a vengeful spectre, he manoeuvred in the darkness to break their will and erase all traces of the revealed truth. His sinister machinations gripped Camille's destiny, threatening to shatter the fragile balance between salvation and oblivion. Every moment spent in this underground world seemed like a mad dash against an invisible trap, striving to drag them into a bottomless abyss. The whispers of the past echoed in every gust of cold wind, reminding Gabriel and Camille that they were but fleeting links in an age-old chain. Their minds ablaze with the passion of discovery, they climbed the steep steps of forgotten knowledge, their hearts beating to the anguished rhythm of this macabre dance on sacred ground. With each step forward, they felt the weight of history bearing down on their shoulders. Yet, their steps did not falter in the face of adversity, armed with the unsinkable hope that burned in their eyes, proud heirs to the flame of the rebels of old.


The shadows in the underground corridors thicken to better engulf the fugitives rushing through them. Gabriel and Camille, as they feverishly examine the ancient documents by the flickering light of a candle, feel the weight of centuries bearing down on their shoulders. Each moment seems to drag them further into an uncertain future, where danger lurks like an insatiable predator. The old papers give off a musty smell of buried secrets, gradually reveal-ing the charred veneer of hidden truths.

Meanwhile, in the putrid labyrinth of the past, Aurélien, Éléonore, and Raphaël dodge the sharp claws of the Count, whose heavy foot-steps echo like ominous sounds. Their shad-ows dance to the rhythm of the flickering torch flames, performing a macabre waltz beneath the damp vaults. Each step, each heartbeat, merges with the sigh of the ancient stones, weaving a web of fear and hope. As the foul vapours of centuries past mingle with the ven-omous threats of Beaumont's descendant, a suffocating atmosphere settles in, oppressing both eras with the same weight.

Questions jostle for answers, filling the saturated air with dark notes and sinister masquerades. Each word discovered in the archives sheds light on an increasingly obscure facet of the poisonous plot hatched over generations. Yet, in the growing shadows of this endless night, hope remains, fragile but tenacious, like a ray of moonlight piercing the stormy clouds. As the trap slowly closes and freedom evaporates like an elusive mirage, resilience finds its voice in the frantic beating of hearts, vibrating in unison with the anxious pulse of Paris. Each moment hastens the inexorable destiny towards a timeless dénouement, where past and present intertwine to better ignite in a final act whose outcome no one can predict.

As Gabriel and Camille made their way through the dark, winding corridors, a growing sense of anxiety gripped them. The flickering light of their flashlights seemed to collide with a dark force, as if the darkness was trying to envelop them. Each step echoed ominously in the underground labyrinth, and the breath of danger could be felt in the air thick with mystery. The documents they had discovered had opened a Pandora's box of financial intrigue, revealing a scandal linked to secret manipulations dating back to the 19th Century. The evidence they had gathered pointed to a truth as unexpected as it was disturbing, fuelling Gabriel's curiosity but also fanning the flames of hidden vengeance.

Meanwhile, in a Machiavellian game orchestrated by Beaumont's descendant, Camille's life was in danger. The shadow of blackmail loomed menacingly, like a grim prophecy waiting to be fulfilled. The fragile thread that connected them both to the light of day seemed ready to snap, giving way to merciless darkness. As the past and present mingled in an inextricable ballet, muffled impulses revealed the duality of human beings: between an insatiable thirst for truth and an ancestral terror of the unknown.

Secrets and lies, buried under layers of time, emerged like spectres thirsty for retribution. Blackmail on the edge of light crystallised the ultimate battle between courage and cowardice, between the desire to shed light on the darkness of the past and the murky threat of eternal silence. The echoes of past lives marked the path of their indelible presence, as fate played with these souls in search of justice. At the heart of this fierce struggle for truth and survival, Gabriel and Camille had to dig deep into their courage to face the blackmail that held their destiny in its diabolical grip. In the darkness, only the glimmer of moral integrity could dispel the shadows of compromise. Their adventure, shaped by temporal intricacies and contemporary perils, would reach its climax in a face-to-face confrontation with the dark forces, defying the silent ultimatum hanging over them.

Muffled screams echoed through the corridors as Gabriel and Camille made their way through the oppressive shadows of the Opera's underground passages. Each step sounded like a sinister echo, bringing them inexorably closer to an uncertain fate. The flickering flames of the torches revealed glimpses of the ancient frescoes on the walls, silent witnesses to the conspiracies perpetrated over the centuries. As they deciphered the documents in their possession, a bitter truth emerged: a financial scandal insidiously linked to the events of the 19th Century was about to be revealed. The yellowed pages of the diaries hinted at the dark ramifications of a centuries-old conspiracy, intertwining the fate of their ancestors with that of today's influential men.

Meanwhile, in a macabre ballet beneath the sleeping capital, the elusive spectres of the past were rising again. Aurélien, Éléonore, and Raphaël were being hunted like fugitives by the Count of Beaumont himself. Their frightened figures wandered through the dark labyrinth, their hearts pounding with fear.

However, the present was not without its own dangers. Beaumont's descendant, through his relentless blackmail, threatened Camille's life, forcing Gabriel to make a heart-wrenching choice: remain silent or see his ally suffer a terrible fate. Faced with this silent ultimatum, an electric tension filled the stale air of the catacombs. Darkness seemed to close in on our heroes, trapping them in a deadly vice where every thought, every gesture, took on vital importance.

The relentless race against time took on tragic proportions, as if time itself, an accomplice to the plots being hatched, had frozen in a macabre tableau. Thus, amid the muffled echoes of ultimatums and ancient secrets, a duel was being fought between cursed legacies and intertwined destinies. As the dying embers of the torches cast dancing shadows, each of the protagonists was faced with a dark trial—that of choosing between resignation and struggle, between silence and revelation. And in this relentless struggle between past and present, between flickering light and threatening darkness, the epic and magnificent tale of those who dared to challenge the chains of time to uncover the truth buried for so long began to unfold.

# 8
# Aurélien's Legacy

In the enchanting darkness of the secret library, Gabriel discovers some shocking letters that shed light on his connection to his ancestors, who have been freed from the dark veil of history. The dusty archives reveal passionate letters and diaries written by Aurélien Desmoulins, testifying to his deep convictions and his fight for justice. In a disturbing twist of fate, each word seems to resonate in Gabriel's tormented soul, like a melody from a distant past. Aurélien's aspirations, doubts, and hopes strangely merge with those of Gabriel, forming an unbreakable bond that transcends time and space.

Through the yellowed pages, hearts beat in unison, emotions intertwine, and the scars of history are revealed. These buried stories bear witness to the nobility and honour of the Desmoulins family, swept away by the turmoil of their time. Aurélien's tragic adventures come to life before Gabriel's eyes, revealing the indelible legacy that unites them across the centuries, like a flickering flame passed down from generation to generation. He feels Aurélien's resilience in the face of adversity, his burning desire to spread light in the heart of darkness, and his timeless quest for justice. The very essence of the Desmoulins family comes to life through these lines, infusing Gabriel with new strength and unexpected clarity. Each word, carefully written in ink, weaves an emotional bond between Gabriel and his ancestor, revealing secrets that have been buried for far too long.

This discovery marks an irreversible turning point in Gabriel's quest for truth, offering him a legacy of meaning and honour. However, with this revelation comes new questions, unexpected challenges, and the heavy responsibility of preserving the integrity of the Desmoulins family. The flickering candlelight illuminates not only the secret library but also the uncertain future of Gabriel, who finds himself unwittingly caught up in a transcendent family saga. In this sanctuary of forgotten knowledge, Gabriel reflects on the visionary strength of his ancestors, ready to carry on their legacy with determination and fervour.

That night, the streets of Paris were steeped in a heavy atmosphere, laden with the weight of ancient deeds that haunted every corner of the city. Gabriel and Camille had ventured into the forgotten tunnels of the Opera House, determined to pierce the veil of mystery that had tormented their existence. As they made their way through the darkness, a strange sense of familiarity washed over Gabriel. The damp walls seemed to whisper long-buried secrets, and the echo of footsteps resonated like a reminder of past generations.

Guided by an indomitable force, they finally discovered a forgotten room filled with remnants of a bygone era. In the centre of the room, a solid wooden table bore the marks of time, adorned with mysterious symbols carved into its worn surface. It was here that destinies crossed, that bonds of blood and honour revealed their true nature.

Through the ages, the descendants of Aurelian, Eleanor, and their companions carried within them the legacy of an unfinished quest: to restore the truth and reestablish the honour of their ancestors. Gabriel felt his heart beat to the rhythm of family legends. At the same time, Camille, illuminated by the flickering light of their lamps, immersed herself in silent contemplation of this timeless room. The voices of the past seemed to echo around them, whispering tales of courage, betrayal, and honourable sacrifices. Every object, every artefact, became a silent witness to forgotten battles, promises kept, and oaths broken.

Faced with this scene frozen in time, Gabriel and Camille realised that their destiny was intimately linked to that of their ancestors, shaped by an age-old struggle for justice and dignity. In the poignant silence of the Parisian night, the flame of their family heritage was rekindled within them, inspiring an indomitable determination. They were ready to face the shadows of the past, to overcome the obstacles that stood in their way, and to honour the memory of the unsung heroes who had given meaning to their existence. In that forgotten room, the weight of honour and ancestral promises became more tangible than ever, igniting their souls with a passion that refused to be forgotten.

The magnificent and enchanting city of Paris was plunged into darkness as Gabriel and Camille ventured into the cobblestone streets. The flickering streetlights cast dancing shadows on the facades of centuries-old buildings, giving the French capital a mystical atmosphere that seemed steeped in a thousand years of history.

On this night when past and present intertwined, the two protagonists felt as if they had been transported to another world, far from the hustle and bustle of modern life. Silence enveloped the city, broken only by the soft murmur of the wind and the muffled footsteps of the lone adventurers. The moonlight dimly illuminated the rooftops of the buildings, offering a fleeting glimpse of the sculptures and ornaments that bore witness to the capital's rich architectural heritage.

As Gabriel and Camille walked on, they felt a strange connection with the past generations who had walked on these same cobblestones, carrying with them the hopes, fears, and heartbreaks of a bygone era. They were aware that their own lives were intimately linked to those of their ancestors, carrying with them the burden of buried secrets and unjustly forgotten tragedies. On this deeply symbolic night, Gabriel's thoughts turned to Aurélien Desmoulins, his heroic ancestor whose courage and determination seemed to manifest themselves through him. He felt the burden of preserving Aurélien's legacy, of bringing the truth to light, and of fulfilling a long-neglected quest for justice.

Camille, meanwhile, shared this deep conviction, feeling that their destinies were closely intertwined with those of Aurélien, Éléonore, and Raphaël, the protagonists of a tragic epic whose final chapters were yet to be written. Guided by an indomitable inner strength, they continued their journey through the nocturnal maze of the City of Light, aware that every street, every bridge, every building held forgotten secrets that could illuminate their path. In the heart of the Parisian night, they were determined to lift the veil on mysteries that had been buried for too long, to exhume the spectres of the past and finally offer redemption to those who had sacrificed their lives for a noble and elusive ideal.


Night had fallen on Paris like a dark canvas, enveloping the city in mystery and danger. In the darkness of the winding alleys, Éléonore's fate hung by a fragile thread, ready to snap at any moment. Hurried footsteps echoed on the damp cobblestones, while her short breath betrayed her anguish. She had narrowly escaped the clutches of betrayal, but the price to pay was heavy, too heavy.

Raphaël's face appeared before her eyes, the man who had dared to defy fate to offer her a chance of survival. In the shadows of the sinister Parisian alleyways, Éléonore frantically searched for a way out, an escape route that would allow her to defy the dark forces hunting her. Memories swirled in her tormented mind, evoking Raphaël's determined gaze, ready to sacrifice everything to protect her.

Her heart bled at the cruel reality of her hasty departure. Still, she knew it was the only way to keep hope alive, the only way to give meaning to this ultimate sacrifice. The alleys finally led her to a hidden door, concealed in the shadows of an old abandoned building. This door, a symbol of freedom, was also the emblem of her painful dilemma. Should she cross the threshold and survive, or stay and face an uncertain fate? Muffled sobs betrayed her inner pain, the intimate struggle between duty and distress. But in the midst of this emotional storm, one thing became clear: Raphaël had given everything for her, and his sacrifice would not be in vain.

Pushing the door open with renewed determination, Éléonore stepped into the unknown, aware that each step brought her closer to the truth, but also to her own demons. The night was her ally in this essential quest for freedom, justice, and the memory of forgotten heroes. Her footsteps echoed in the darkness, marking the path of resistance, guided by the flame of those courageous souls who had sacrificed everything for an ideal greater than life itself.

The hours passed in oppressive anxiety in that dark prison where time seemed to stand still. Éléonore stood there, each breath a cruel reminder of her isolation. In the darkness of her cell, she felt the weight of betrayal and sacrifice hanging over her shoulders. Each moment robbed her of a piece of her strength and determination, but deep down, a glimmer of hope continued to burn within her. Suddenly, a distant noise broke the ominous silence. She recognised the familiar sound of Raphaël's footsteps approaching. Their eyes met through the bars, and without a word, a silent understanding passed between them. The seconds seemed like an eternity as they devised a daring plan for her freedom. In a burst of courage and determination, Raphaël created a diversion, drawing the guards away from Éléonore's cell. Taking advantage of this moment of inattention, she seized the opportunity with renewed boldness.

The key turned in the lock, the door creaked seductively as it swung open, and she darted into the dark corridor, where darkness embraced every corner. Her escape was like a wild dance with destiny, under the watchful eye of the moon, silently watching over her attempt to escape the shackles of oppression. Her footsteps echoed until she found refuge in the protective shadows of the Parisian underground, where each echo of her footsteps seemed to whisper the memories of those who had fought before her.

Guided by this indomitable inner strength, she continued her quest for freedom, aware that each step into the unknown was also a step towards the light. The night wind whispered promises of renewal as she ran toward the glimmer of hope that shone at the end of the darkness. Éléonore had freed herself from her physical chains, but her true escape was only just beginning. Her mind ablaze with determination, she felt bound by an eternal promise of honour and bravery, ready to defy fate to claim her rightful place in history.


The shadows of night enveloped Paris in a mysterious veil. In this theatre of intrigue, a tragic ballet unfolded, where every gesture, every breath carried the weight of destiny. In the heart of the forgotten underground passages, Raphaël stood facing a decision with far-reaching consequences, like a figure from ancestral tales. His gaze, marked by fierce determination, was lost in the darkness that threatened to engulf him. Still, his soul remained anchored in a decision he sensed was inevitable. The trajectory of his existence was irrevocably converging on a choice that would shake the very foundations of his own history.

Between love and duty, between loyalty and freedom, he stood there, alone in the face of his destiny. Fate seemed to bend under the weight of this frozen scene, as if time had suspended its flight to take full awareness of the crucial stakes being played out in the shadows of the catacombs. As the distant echoes of his pursuers' footsteps rang ominously against the stone walls, illuminating the threat hanging over their escape, Raphaël did not hesitate. In a gesture marked by nobility and sacrifice, he whispered to Éléonore to flee from this hell, thus sealing the fate of their shared destiny. His heroic commitment defined a tragic parable in which each protagonist, charged with an intimate force, had to face their own demons and offer the world the heartbreaking spectacle of their most profound dilemmas. His gesture, like an act of moral alchemy, transmuted cowardice into bravery, fear into daring, imbuing the epic tale of this cursed lineage with unexpected transcendence. For in the darkness, he sketched the contours of an immortal legend, forged not by victory, but by selfless sacrifice.

At the edge of destiny, in a final act of generosity, Raphaël embraced the sacrificial role that had fallen to him, offering humanity the living testament of an unsung hero. And while the footsteps of the deceitful incarnations of treason echoed through the labyrinth of corridors, his image remained, like an indelible relic, engraved in the annals of centuries to come.

Raphaël rushed forward with incredible bravery, split the darkness and confronted Beaumont's descendant without the slightest hesitation. Silence fell in the dark tunnel; only the panting breath of the protagonists echoed among the ancient vaults. With eyes sparkling with defiance, Beaumont's descendant was taken aback by Raphaël's audacity. The two men faced each other, carrying within them all the weight of a lineage marked by betrayal and loyalty, by shadow and light. Gabriel and Camille remained frozen, enveloped by the palpable tension emanating from this timeless confrontation. Echoes of the past seemed to vibrate through the ancient stones, accompanying this silent duel between the descendants of a troubled history, ready to close an ancestral chapter laden with unspoken secrets.

The descendant of Beaumont, distraught, was unable to hide his turmoil. Decades of denial clashed with Raphaël's fierce determination, like a renunciation of an unbearable legacy. Guilt hung indelibly over his shoulders, while the legacy of his ancestors seemed to condemn him to perpetuate a dark tradition. His averted gaze betrayed his resignation to the truth that was about to be revealed to the world. Faced with this upheaval, Gabriel suddenly understood the profound significance of the story unfolding before his astonished eyes. He realised that his own destiny was intimately linked to this epic confrontation, as if circumstances had woven an implacable plot to propel him into the heart of a hereditary mandate. The remains of Aurelian seemed to whisper ancient words, reminding him that he, too, was an unwitting player in a family saga with unexpected ramifi-cations.

Meanwhile, in a discreet corner of the tunnel, Éléonore silently watched the confrontation unfold, her face marked by contained emotion. She had survived the tragedy thanks to Raphaël's sacrifice, a silent bond that sealed their shared destiny. Her mind burned with a secret fire, determined to restore the honour of her ancestral family. This confrontation, an allegory of past torments, resonated like a final act of retribution for all the suffering endured. Soon, an unexpected way out emerged from the darkness, revealing an unexplored passage to forgotten depths, plunging each of the heirs into an unfathomable abyss, but one tinged with hope. A new era was dawning, crowned by the confrontation of intertwined destinies, ready to reveal secrets that had been buried for too long.

Gabriel scanned the darkness of this new tunnel with a mixture of fascination and apprehension. Accompanied by Camille, he advanced step by step, lighting their way with an ancient lantern found among the forgotten artefacts of the Opera House. The stone walls seemed to whisper secrets lost for centuries, and the heavy atmosphere appeared to carry the weight of many past tragedies. As their footsteps echoed in the oppressive silence of the underground passages, Gabriel felt an undeniable connection to his ancestor Aurélien. He now understood that justice was their shared legacy. This quest transcended time and took shape through the puzzles and mysteries they encountered during their exploration.

As they progressed, ancient murals, almost erased by time, began to appear. They revealed epic scenes, moments frozen in history, which seemed to narrate the exploits of the characters who had once walked these same corridors. One of these paintings, particularly striking, depicted a spectacular escape, a courageous flight into the heart of darkness, evoking Raphaël's sacrifice to allow Éléonore to continue the fight. Overwhelmed by the intensity of this discovery, Gabriel couldn't help but imagine the distress and heroism of his distant ancestors. These vanished faces, with their tragic destinies, suddenly came to life through these silent works, silent witnesses to an unfinished epic.

Then, as the flickering flames of the lantern illuminated a hidden passage behind a cracked wall, Gabriel realised that the light he had glimpsed through the thick shadows was much more than a mere metaphor. It was the promise of a buried truth. This dazzling clarity would break the chains of the past and finally reveal the close ties between the present and the long-forgotten. In the excitement of this imminent discovery, Gabriel felt that each step brought him closer not only to solving the mystery that had haunted his family for generations but also to the redemption of the mourning souls who still wandered in the hidden corners of history. Now the tunnel stretched out before them, an ancient path paved with promises and revelations, ready to guide them to a truth they could no longer escape.

As Gabriel and Camille venture deeper into the newly discovered tunnel, a feeling of excitement mixed with apprehension washes over them. The darkness seemed to envelop them in mystery, but a distant glow caught their eyes, promising an imminent revelation. Their footsteps echoed on the damp stone, punctuated by ancestral echoes that seemed to whisper secrets buried for too long. As they advanced, the walls of the tunnel seemed to close in, as if to hold their breath. The atmosphere becomes heavy, laden with forgotten memories and intertwined destinies. Gabriel feels an inner strength rising within him, as if his ancestor's aspirations were echoing in him, pushing him towards this final revelation.

Suddenly, the growing light illuminates the narrow passageway and reveals a striking sight: an underground chamber emerges from the darkness, like a relic from the past offered up to the amazed eyes of the explorers. The vaults decorated with enigmatic symbols and the remains of a forgotten artefact give this place a magical aura, reinforcing the link between the present and the past. As Gabriel and Camille explore this forgotten sanctuary, every detail seems to whisper a greater truth, an epic tale buried in the depths of time. The objects around them tell a story of struggle and resilience, a legacy forged in adversity and passed down through the generations. The discovery of this sacred place stirs deep emotions within them, a mixture of respect and humility for the sacrifices made for noble ideals. Through the centuries, the aspirations of these valiant souls have endured trials and tribulations, finally finding refuge in the flickering light of this forgotten room. Guided by an indomitable will, Gabriel and Camille know that this revelation marks the end of a quest, but also the beginning of a new legacy. They sense that the echoes of this eternal promise will resonate for a long time to come, reminding future generations of the price of freedom and the power of ideals that transcend time.

When Gabriel and Camille entered the previously unknown tunnel, a sense of ancient mystery enveloped them. The walls seemed to whisper secrets, and the wind blowing through the passages echoed like a call from the past. In the darkness, their flashlights cast dancing shadows that seemed to tell a forgotten story, a story whose outcome Gabriel did not yet know. He felt that each step brought him closer to the truth, but also to his destiny. The tunnel turned out to be much more than a simple underground passageway. It was the very symbol of Aurélien's legacy, a legacy of courage, passion, and determination. Every stone, every turn, bore the indelible mark of this distant ancestor, a silent witness to the trials endured in the name of justice.

Gabriel felt an echo of this commitment in his own actions, as if the blood of the Desmoulins still flowed through his veins, pulsing with the rhythm of an eternal promise. As they continued on their way, a thought occurred to Gabriel: life was a series of choices, sacrifices, and hopes. Like Raphaël, who had sacrificed his own freedom to allow Éléonore to escape, everyone had to face the twists and turns of fate. The path to the light was not without obstacles, and sometimes sacrifices had to be made to preserve what was essential. This reflection prompted him to look at Camille with renewed gratitude, recognising in her a valuable ally in this unique quest.

Finally, as they advanced, a distant glow appeared, fragile and shimmering. It was a promise of hope, an invitation to lift the veil on secrets that had been buried for too long. Emotion overwhelmed Gabriel as he sensed the imminence of the long-awaited revelation. In the semi-darkness, he saw Aurélien again, a prisoner of his time, but fearlessly bound to him by unspoken ties. Through the centuries, their destinies were intimately intertwined, united by the unchanging quest for justice.

Thus, in this tunnel laden with symbols and emotions, Gabriel felt a deep sense of accomplishment growing within him. He now understood that the eternal promise was to honour the sacrifices of the past, to break the chains of injustice, and to give history a conclusion worthy of its heroes. The echoes of a forgotten era resonated within him like an ancient melody, heralding the imminent triumph of truth. And it was with this certainty, guided by the flame of courage inherited from his ancestors, that he stepped forward, ready to welcome the nourishing light of knowledge.

# 9
# The Truth Comes Out

Dawn breaks over the City as the media prepares to reveal the hidden legacy of the Desmoulins and Beaumont families. The first rays of sunlight paint the facades of Parisian buildings in a golden hue, heralding an exceptional day when the truth will finally be revealed. In the press offices, sharp-minded journalists are busy piecing together the scattered pieces of a long-hidden historical puzzle. The anticipated revelations are rekindling public interest in the mysteries buried beneath the Paris Opera House. Everyone is holding their breath in feverish anticipation, while the City itself seems to be pulsing with impatience. The pressure of political and historical stakes is palpable, as if the fate of an entire lineage hinged on this crucial moment.

Through the foggy streets of the capital, an electrifying anticipation spreads, heralding a day that will go down in history. In the media corridors, the excitement is palpable. Whispered conversations and secretive glances fuel the tense atmosphere as the long-awaited revelation draws near. The screens in the newsrooms are already flickering with the first glimpses of the truth, which is about to break the chains of silence. Hope and fear mingle in everyone's hearts, for the harsh light of disclosure can both illuminate and consume.

On this day blessed by the gods of history, the intertwined destinies of the Desmoulins and Beaumont families are about to be written in a new chapter, tearing away the stubborn veil that has obscured their memory. It is in this morning mist that the contours of a forgotten saga take shape, ready to breathe new life into a history frozen in darkness.

When the first lines of the forgotten stories emerged from the shadows and stepped into the light, it was as if the veil of time had been torn away before the incredulous eyes of the world. The ancient words danced across the yellowed pages, revealing captivating stories of courage, loyalty, and sacrifice, carefully buried in the depths of oblivion. Each story unveiled depicted a bygone era, a time when destinies were woven into political intrigues and devious plots. Readers discovered unsung heroes, their unique qualities emerging from the pages like glimmers of hope in a society that had long forgotten their exploits. The truth, long stifled by the weight of lies and manipulation, now shone brightly, setting the hearts of those who dared to listen ablaze.

The world held its breath as it explored the stories, marvelling at the indomitable bravery of the once-oppressed figures. Each line re-vealed was a promise of redemption, a glimmer of humanity that would transcend the centuries. The stories offered a captivating glimpse into a tumultuous era, highlighting the resilience of souls in the face of oppression and injustice.

The press, hungry for truth and justice, eagerly seized upon the stories, bringing the forgotten heroes to life. Newspapers echoed the forgotten testimonies, offering the public a masterful dive into the mysteries of history. Each article rekindled the flame of knowledge and shed light on the grey areas that had fuelled myths and mysteries for generations. In every home, the stories that were revealed became lively topics of conversation, sparking heated debates about truth and responsibility.

The impact of the stories quickly transcended borders, finding an echo in the hearts of those seeking redemption for forgotten heroes. Thus, the stories that were revealed brought about a profound transformation in society, inspiring a renewed belief in the power of truth and justice. They paved the way for a collective renaissance, propelling the protagonists from the shadows to their well-deserved status as symbols of bravery and determination. Their forgotten deeds were brought back to life in the present, weaving an invisible thread between generations and reminding the world that the truth, long buried and denied, always emerges with unparalleled power.

The stories that came to light caused a media uproar, disrupting the tranquillity of the Opera and shaking the foundations of history. Journalists, like wild animals thirsty for truth, rushed through the corridors once haunted by conspiracies. Their pens sharpened, ready to tear away the veil of oblivion, blurred the boundaries of time to expose the unsuspected ramifications of the thousand-year-old intrigue.

Fiery editorials filled the columns of daily newspapers, which had long remained silent on the mysteries buried beneath the Opera House. Television reports captured the excitement of Parisians, now aware that their footsteps were following in the footsteps of a hidden history. The media clamour stirred up forgotten memories, echoing through the ages to reach the minds of an entire people. Spurred on by the revelations, renowned academics set about unravelling the tangled web of the past and present. Their meticulous analyses, seemingly more intertwined than the symbols engraved on the walls of the secret chamber, shed light on the murky paths of forgotten destinies.

Historians, armed with their authoritative pens, offered a new dimension to the epic tale told by the dusty stones of the Opera House, inspiring everyone to believe in the existence of a forgotten part of humanity. Through literary and artistic tributes, the media clamour brought back to life characters condemned to oblivion.

Poets celebrated the resilience of heroes confined to the darkness of the centuries, and painters created paintings haunted by faces faded by time. This creative effervescence, tinged with fervent admiration, wove an immutable web around figures once condemned to oblivion. Emanating from looks marked by respect and gratitude, a sense of reparation floated in the air, like a promise—a promise to perpetuate the memory of those who dared to confront unacknowledged oppression. Thus, the media clamour turned into collective veneration for those whose deeds defied oblivion, giving the Opera a lasting soul, forged in the infinite forge of legends.

The calm before the storm had offered a moment of respite to all of Paris. The media clamour, like a rumbling thunder, heralded the imminent outbreak of the truth. The stories that were revealed, like moths emerging from the darkness, aroused fascination and fear. In this electric atmosphere, the eyes of the world turned to a long-forgotten past, where valiant souls and sinister conspiracies echoed.

Then came the long-awaited moment when

every word spoken and every line printed set free the truth that had been held captive for too long. The forgotten heroes regained their lustre, emerging from the veil of oblivion to claim the righteousness of their actions. Like distant shadows caught up by the light, their names were held high, bearing redemption and honour.

The pages of history, once stained by slander and malice, were freed from an unjust yoke. Figures once marked by courage and devotion shone once more, animated by the restorative breath of public recognition. Their exploits, once relegated to the confines of memory, were brought back to life under the bright spotlight of the media, dazzling witnesses to this resurrection of glory. In the face of this triumphant revelation, the shame that had tainted their actions was swept away like the mists of a new dawn.

The voices of those who had dared to slander them were silenced by the irrefutable force of truth. At the same time, the nobility of the heroes regained their rightful place in the pantheon of the great men and women of their time. Thus, in the grandiose shadow of the Parisian monuments, theatres of past intrigues and intertwined destinies, the forgotten protagonists of this saga sought refuge. Where they had once been banished, convinced that they would be buried forever in the depths of oblivion, they were now welcomed as heroes, acclaimed, adored, and revered by a grateful crowd. And the lifeblood of memory flowed once more through their veins, rekindling the sacred fire of collective memory.

The revelation of these long-hidden truths broadened the horizons of the public mind, revealing the complexity of human greatness and torment. Thus, thanks to these memorable events, a sumptuous fresco emerged, in which bravery, ingenuity, and loyalty found their place amid darkness and treachery. And as the resounding echo of the revealed truths rang out, the very destiny of Paris was clarified, engraved forever in the brilliant annals of its history.

Following the revelation of compromising documents highlighting the malicious acts perpetrated by Beaumont's descendant, the heavy atmosphere surrounding the Paris Opera thickens. Muffled whispers and accusing glances multiply, casting a shadow over the ancestral prestige of the Beaumont family.

Faced with the sensational revelations reported in the press, Parisian Society is shaken to its core. The descendant of Beaumont, once respected for his noble title and colossal fortune, sees his mask crack under the crushing weight of the truth. His once haughty features are now marked by fear and humiliation, betraying his tormented soul. Allegations of intrigue and pernicious financial manipulation spread like wildfire, consuming the family's reputation. Damning accounts splattered the immaculate columns of the ancestral mansion, tarnishing the once-spotless image of the local hero.

The disgrace of Beaumont's descendant seems irreparable, freezing his fate in the infamous annals of history. In this social cataclysm, the thrill-seeking public watches with fascination as arrogance and tyranny, hidden behind a mask of respectability, inevitably fall. Everyone holds their breath, witnessing the relentless justice looming on the horizon, ready to restore the balance broken by so many years of hidden oppression. As Beaumont's descendant sinks into the torturous depths of shame and guilt, the shadows of the past resurface, those of the unsung heroes who once endured the torments of injustice. Through this merciless revelation, the dark history of the Beaumont family is laid bare, offering a precious opportunity to pay tribute to the forgotten victims and honour the courage of the protagonists, forever etched in the memory of a tumultuous era.

The descendant of Beaumont, once an

all-powerful monarch, sees his empire of lies collapse under the relentless weight of justice. His contorted face betrays an anguish hitherto hidden behind a mask of arrogant confidence. The heavens themselves seemed to tremble, their bright rays filtering through the half-open shutters and casting an unreal atmosphere over the scene of the drama. His hands shook, powerless in the icy grip of the handcuffs that, like a symbol of his inexorable downfall, closed around his wrists. The aura of mystery and power he had cultivated for so long was crumbling, revealing the truth hidden behind his schemes. All around him, the effervescent buzz of the press and spectators who had come to witness the inevitable indictment formed a backdrop testifying to the restored sovereignty of justice.

Whispers spread the story of his misdeeds, filling the room with vengeful talk and sharp murmurs. At that moment, the silence freezes, as if to better highlight the resounding brilliance of his imminent downfall. His eyes, once filled with arrogance and defiance, now reflect a flickering light tinged with palpable terror. Faced with the irrefutable evidence and the restored credibility of the heroes whose reputations he tried to sully, he seems to realise with horror that his sins are about to catch up with him. Behind the bars of his own treachery, he can no longer escape the sentence that awaits him, like a leading actor overtaken by the shadows of his own tragedy.

The cobbled street suddenly seemed hostile, the facades of the majestic buildings appearing doomed to be silent witnesses to his downfall. In the distance, the tumult of the City appeared to engulf him, rushing him inexorably toward his fate as his own actions resurfaced like spectres weighing him down with their ominous foreboding. Beyond the closed doors and tightly locked windows, a new era was dawning, resonating with the brilliance of justice finally being served.

As the truth comes to light, a revelation transcending the centuries unites destinies separated by the veil of time. The opening of the secret tunnel becomes a gateway between two eras, inviting the present to delve into the depths of the past. The artefacts found whisper forgotten tales, intertwined stories that connect the lives of yesterday with those of today. Each object exudes an air of mystery, a silent testimony to the struggles and triumphs of those who dared to stand up against oppression. The unearthed archives hold priceless treasures, revealing lost battles and little-known victories. The names of heroes hidden by the mists of time shine once more, illuminating the darkness that had engulfed them.

With delicacy, historians untangle the tangled threads of injustice to weave a living tapestry, vibrant with the courage and determination of those who opposed oppressive forces. Each step in the tunnel resonates like a vibrant echo, a mystical dialogue between the souls of the 19th Century and those of the 21st Century. Visitors, moved by this communion with the past, contemplate the vestiges of history with respect and deep empathy.

The faces frozen in the daguerreotypes regain a silent voice that will carry through future generations, reminding the men and women of today of the universal lessons of bravery and integrity. In this place sanctified by memory, remembrance awakens and blossoms, weaving an indelible web that disturbs and inspires the present. Each fragment of the past rekindles a spark in the eyes of our contemporaries, reminding them that the struggles for justice are timeless. The depth of these historical roots infuses a new understanding, a heightened sensitivity to the tragic vicissitudes and glorious triumphs that have forged our human community. Thus, the archway opening onto the past becomes a hymn to human resilience, an imperishable symphony composed of the discordant notes of ancient conflicts and the emerging harmonies of redemption.

The evening of the revelation had finally arrived. The opera house was plunged into semi-darkness, the tension palpable, when a solemn silence fell over the audience. The musicians, under the expert direction of the renowned conductor, carefully adjusted their instruments. The audience, composed of influential figures, art lovers, and curious onlookers who had come to witness an unprecedented event, held their breath, captivated by the anticipation of this symphony so carefully preserved by time. The curtain rose slowly, revealing a stage whose magnificence dazzled the audience. In the centre stood a vintage grand piano, recently restored for this unique moment. It was the instrument that had carried Aurélien's immortal notes, the same ones that had survived the oblivion and silence imposed by history.

The first movement rang out in the hall, transporting the audience into a whirlwind of emotions. The complex melodies, tinged with passion and rebellion, seemed to bring the protagonists of this forgotten story back to life. Each instrument, each note played by the orchestra, told the story of Aurélien and his companions' struggle for freedom and justice. A transcendent force seemed to permeate the work, reminding us that music could be much more than mere entertainment, but a cry from the heart. This silent protest transcended the ages.

The long-awaited climax sent vibrations through the air. As the last note faded into a poignant echo, a meditative silence enveloped the hall. Then, a thunderous applause erupted, a sign of universal recognition. Faces wet with tears betrayed the intense emotions stirred by this moment, where past and present merged in a musical apotheosis. The symphony of justice, shaped by the pen and genius of Aurélien Desmoulins, had come to an end in a vibrant tribute. The audience realised that this music was much more than a simple composition; it was a testimony to a real struggle, that of humanity against injustice and tyranny. On that day, Aurélien's talent finally regained its place in the firmament of art, illuminating the Paris Opera with a new light, imbued with truth and resilience.

The announcement of the public performance of Aurélien's music resonated throughout the City, attracting music lovers, historians, and the curious. The Opera House, long a silent theatre of past intrigues, was about to reveal to the world the forgotten work of a cursed composer. The hall slowly filled, the palpable tension floating in the air like a suspended note.

Time seemed to stretch, leaving the audience captive in solemn anticipation. The lights gradually dimmed, plunging everyone into expectant darkness. Then, in absolute silence, the orchestra began Aurélien's symphony. Each note seemed to carry within it the suffering of a troubled era, the dashed hopes and buried dreams. The musicians brought the forgotten score to life, a complex melody weaving a thread between past and present. The audience was swept away by this musical cascade, transported into a whirlwind of emotions and memories.

As the music unfolded, faces lit up, some letting slip tears of joy, others revealing smiles tinged with melancholy. It was as if each note awakened the dormant collective memory, reviving forgotten struggles, unrecognised sacrifices, and lost ideals. Aurélien's symphony became the anthem of a quest for truth and justice, transcending mere musical pleasure to become the symbol of a long-awaited rebirth. When the last notes faded into the echoes of the hall, a respectful silence lingered, as if everyone were holding their breath, seeking to prolong the precious moment.

Then came the ovation, a thunderous applause that filled the Opera House, expressing gratitude, recognition, and renewed pride. The forgotten heroes were celebrated and honoured by this music, immortalising their heroic deeds. The audience rose as one, saluting not only the artists on stage, but also the figures from the past brought back to life by this masterful symphony. The evening ended in an atmosphere of renewal.

Lively conversations focused on the rediscovery of this forgotten chapter of history and the triumph of truth over oblivion. Bonds were formed between strangers, uniting hearts around this symphony of justice, which had struck a chord deep within each and every one of them. At that moment, the Opera House became a sanctuary of shared memory, where the echoes of a past too long hidden still resounded. And in this symphony, the great "revelation" was that justice transcends time, healing the wounds of history and paying tribute to the courageous souls who dared to defy oppression.

The day of the revelation brought with it a mix of thrills and intense emotions. Before a vast crowd, forgotten stories resurfaced like a treasure long buried in the depths of time. Confessions of carefully concealed past conspiracies were now laid bare, shedding harsh light on the dark intrigues of the 19th Century.

The press echoed these long-hidden truths, delighting in uncovering the threads woven by secrecy and corrupt power. Honour was finally restored to the unjustly defamed heroes who had been cast into the shadows for decades. Their names shone once again, honoured as they deserved. The descendants of the free-thinking resistance fighters regained their pride, often passed down from generation to generation under the weight of secrecy. In a whirlwind of conflicting emotions, faces wrinkled by time lit up in the glow of this long-awaited rehabilitation. The clamour for justice echoed through the streets.

Meanwhile, Beaumont's descendant, whose mask had finally fallen, found himself facing his own judgment. His once haughty and arrogant face withered in a final, bitter defeat. Inevitable arrest awaited him, like a greedy blade closing in on the man who believed himself untouchable forever.

In this rush of truth, a fascinating symbol emerged: the secret tunnel, long guarded by the shadows of the opera house, was now open to the public. Shrouded in mystery and forgotten history, this space, once steeped in conspiracy and hidden struggles, now offered a welcoming passageway to knowledge and understanding. Visitors flocked to discover this place, steeped in revealed secrets, a tangible symbol of this renewed shared memory.

Finally, still carried by this breath from the past, Aurélien's work came to life under the nimble fingers of a prestigious orchestra. Its powerful and captivating notes rose through the hall, carrying the strength of convictions and ideals that had been stifled for too long.

This symphony paid tribute to the magnificent heroes who had once again become the beacons of an era when the fight for freedom still resonated. That day marked an unshakeable milestone in history, an indelible mark on the collective consciousness. The shared memory between past and present was reborn from its ashes, forged by evidence of courage and intertwined destinies. The revelation of conspiracies, the rehabilitation of the righteous, the opening of the tunnel, and the triumphant music merged to shape a memorable legacy, transforming these once-shadowed heroes into eternal figures of hope and resilience.

# 10
# The Symphony Of Secrets Revealed

Morning light illuminates the reborn Opera House, a symbol of hope. As day breaks over the City of Paris, an exceptional event is being prepared behind the majestic scenes of the Opera House. The first rays of sunlight stream through the large windows, delicately caressing the centuries-old stone walls. The atmosphere is charged with palpable emotion, tinged with a breath of history and renewal.

Guests slowly arrive, dressed in their finest attire, as if paying homage to the ghosts of the past who watch over this iconic building. In the sumptuous hall, whispers mingle with the muffled sound of footsteps, creating a harmonious melody that rises like an offering to the grandeur of the renovated Opera House. Finally, the long-awaited moment arrives. The doors slowly open, revealing the dazzling splendour of the main hall. The chandeliers sparkle with a thousand lights, illuminating every corner of this space once tarnished by the shadows of secrecy.

The guests hold their breath, marvelling at the transformation of this place steeped in history. On stage, an almost sacred solemnity emanates from the precise gestures of the craftsmen, artists, and restorers who have combined their talents to breathe new life into this place. Every detail seems carefully thought out, orchestrating a breathtaking visual spectacle, a vibrant testimony to this unexpected rebirth. The hearts of the audience beat as one, carried away by the indescribable emotion that fills the room as the Opera unfolds its wings like a phoenix rising from the ashes.

As the ceremony progresses, the murmurs turn into cheers, a fleeting but exhilarating symphony in honour of this iconic venue, a true cultural gem. Faces light up with knowing smiles, for everyone present knows that they are participating in a unique moment, a page of history being turned before their eyes, dazzled by the Opera House's restored splendour. This event, with its transformative power, inspires awe, appreciation, and reflection on cultural heritage and historical truth.

The first rays of a new dawn illuminate the majestic façade of the Paris Opera House, a shining symbol of a long-awaited rebirth. The rehabilitation ceremony begins with a solemn murmur, imbued with respect for the vestiges of the past. Under the soft kiss of the morning light, the gilding that adorns the grand foyer sparkles like twinkling stars, silent witnesses to buried secrets and intertwined destinies. The atmosphere is filled with subtle emotion, where every step echoes like a tribute to those who shaped the history of this illustrious institution.

The guests gather in the majestic auditorium, where the distant echoes of enchanting melodies that once captivated souls still linger. Their gazes are lost in the infinite splendour of the frescoes that adorn the ceiling, contemplating a kaleidoscope of scenes frozen in time, silent witnesses to forgotten dramas, passions, and struggles. All around, the delicate lace of the carved balustrades seems to weave a timeless link between generations, offering its benevolent embrace to those who dare to defy oblivion. Beyond the gleaming panelling, voices rise to deliver speeches imbued with solemnity. Each word resonates like an iridescent soap bubble, reflecting the fires of the soul and the brilliance of long-hidden truths. The scars of oppression are thus exposed to the light of truth, magnified by the evocative power of words that echo in the hearts of those gathered. The emotion is palpable, as hope is reborn like a resplendent phoenix, bearing a promise of renewal and reconciliation with a past that has been hidden for too long.

Then, as a counterpoint to these meaningful words, music begins to fill the sacred space. The notes rise slowly, spreading their diaphanous wings to caress the assembled spirits. This is the magic of art, transcendent and eternal, playing with darkness to infuse every fibre of the soul with vibrant poetry. The melodies resonate like tributes to forgotten heroes, lost loves, and ideals that have fallen into oblivion. They vibrate with infinite tenderness and unexpected strength, rekindling the strained bonds between the living and the ghosts of the past. And then, as the last notes seem to dissolve into the still air, a moment suspended in time comes to an end. The ceremony fades gently, giving way to a fragile but magnificent promise: that of a future forged in the communion of memories, where the Paris Opera spreads its wings as the timeless guardian of beauty, truth, and grace.

Silence fell in the richly decorated reception hall. Gabriel, standing beside Camille, gazed with emotion at the gilded decorations and frescoes of a bygone era, silent witnesses to the events that had turned their lives upside down. The guests, dressed in their finest attire, had gathered to witness a historic moment, a ceremony steeped in symbolism and redemption. Under the warm glow of the antique chandeliers, a solemn atmosphere filled the room. Gabriel felt a deep sense of responsibility to pay tribute to those who had fought in the shadows for truth and justice.

Standing up, he looked at the assembly with determined eyes and began his speech. He recounted with passion the fascinating discoveries that had marked their investigation, evoking the workings of a thousand-year-old conspiracy hidden beneath the vaults of the Opera House. Each word seemed to weave an invisible thread between the present and the past, bringing together the destinies of similar characters despite the centuries that separated them. He paid tribute to Aurélien and Éléonore, to their courage and resilience in the face of adversity, striking a chord in the hearts of the audience. Then came the long-awaited moment when the secrets that had been buried for too long would finally be revealed.

Gabriel unveiled the ancient documents, coded musical scores, and diaries to the audience, indisputable evidence of a conspiracy hatched in the shadows of opulent lodges. Whispers of astonishment rippled through the audience as faces filled with amazement and emotion at the revelation of so many mysteries. The symbiosis between past and present reached its peak. Gabriel's speech echoed the struggles of the past, vibrating in the electrified atmosphere of the reception hall. Each of the guests seemed to carry the weight of the revelations on their shoulders, aware that they were not just spectators, but active participants in a historic moment whose echoes would resonate through the ages. In the end, light triumphed over darkness, illuminating the once-dark corners of the Paris Opera's history. Gabriel concluded his speech by urging the assembly to preserve the memory of the events that had just been revealed, to pass on the torch of vigilance and truth to future generations.

A thunderous applause greeted his final words, testifying to everyone's gratitude for this introspective quest that had transcended time and space. The breath of history exhaled its notes in the majestic walls of the Opera House, as if the old stones themselves were vibrating to the rhythm of a long-buried symphony.

The rehabilitation ceremony engraved in the collective memory the triumph of truth over darkness and the uncovering of the mysteries of the past. Under the sparkling chandeliers, Gabriel Moreau stood alongside Camille Fournier, united by this adventure that had taken them on a quest to the ends of time. Their eyes meet those of the guests, a harmonious mix of history buffs and curious minds eager for new discoveries. The speeches resonate like powerful chords, revealing the secret struggles and sacrifices buried for so many years. The echo of the words fills the space, showing the greatness of the souls who dared to face adversity to defend universal ideals. Through the twists and turns of the narrative, the audience is transported into a whirlwind of emotions, oscillating between admiration and amazement at the strength of the protagonists, both past and present.

Then comes the long-awaited moment when the veil is lifted from the once-hidden tunnel. Like a rainbow after a storm, it unfolds before the astonished eyes of the audience, revealing not only ancient stones but also testimonies of lives marked by an intense quest for freedom. Each object on display seems to whisper its story, plunging visitors into a journey out of time, rooted in the reality of the past. Gabriel and Camille lose themselves in this museum of resurrected memory, captivated by the traces of their predecessors. In each relic, they discern a distant echo of their own struggle for the revelation of truth. The scattered pieces of the puzzle come together to create a striking picture, revealing the precious legacy passed down from generation to generation. As the discovery unfolds, a symphony rises, blending the voices of the past and the present, composing an ode to perseverance and justice.

It is then, in this setting of knowledge and renewal, that the last page of Aurélien's journal is solemnly unfolded. His ancestral words echo through the space, evoking a palpable and pure emotion. Glances are exchanged, carrying the weight of heritage and the pride of knowing that history will never again be frozen in the shadows. Finally, the last chord resounds, carrying this shining truth, sealing forever the memory of those who shaped the future in the discreet folds of the past.

The gilding of the Opera House shone once again in the sunlight, as if to celebrate a long-awaited rebirth. The restoration ceremony was a solemn occasion, filled with palpable emotion. The guests, dressed in their finest attire, now strolled through the restored corridors of this cultural landmark, steeped in the long and turbulent history that had seen them come into being. Under the majestic vaulted ceiling, conversations murmured like hymns celebrating the glorious past of this iconic building. Every step, every glance was imbued with symbolic meaning, like an offering to the stones that had stood the test of time. The breath of centuries rushed through the newly reclaimed spaces, breathing new life into them, tinged with the ancient chords that had shaped destinies.

The inauguration of the museum, heir to the hidden tunnel, was like an initiation rite. Visitors wandered around with eager curiosity, contemplating the patiently restored artefacts, silent witnesses to a distant era. The shadows of illustrious figures seemed to dance to the sound of footsteps, offering the present a glimpse of a past rich in intrigue and mystery. Each display case, each painting whispered its own story, captivating the minds of the daring explorers of the present. Gabriel and Camille, hand in hand, moved among the bustling crowds, sharing a renewed intimacy. Their eyes met, filled with unspeakable meaning, as if the thread of past events had woven indissoluble bonds between them. Through the rooms magnified by the soft light, they perceived echoes of the trials they had overcome and the truths they had unearthed, feeling how much the quest had transformed them.

The last page of Aurélien's diary, carried by a light breeze, seemed to float in the air like a final offering, a promise of a legacy perpetuated through time. This silent reading resonated like a closing song, that of an adventure which, although over, remained alive in their memories. And as the last notes of the ancient music faded away, the restored harmony enveloped the Opera House in an aura of renewed grandeur, honouring those who had dedicated themselves body and soul to illuminating the troubled paths of history.

Gabriel and Camille stood in the centre of the Opera House, silent witnesses to a rebirth in which they had played a privileged role. The newly erected museum was much more than a collection of ancient objects; it was a reflection of their incredible odyssey through the twists and turns of time.

Every stone, every musical score, every relic exuded memories woven in the darkness of centuries. Under the majestic vaulted ceiling, the voices of ancestors seemed to whisper, infusing the atmosphere with mystery and wonder. Gabriel, his eyes filled with emotion, felt a hand slip gently into his, and when he met Camille's gaze, he saw the depth of their unbreakable bond. It was through an ancestral mystery that their destinies had crossed, merging into a perfect symphony. The trials they had endured had forged strong bonds between them, etched into the swirls of time. While the crowd enjoyed themselves around them, their connection transcended dimensions, capable of defying the passing of time. The silent company of their ancestors seemed to approve, as if the echoes of their history harmoniously blended with the present.

Beyond the vicissitudes of time, Gabriel and Camille were now the guardians of an immortal legacy, united by a quest that had led them where no one else had dared to venture. Their souls vibrated in unison, replaying the distant melodies that sealed their shared destiny. Then, in the hushed silence of this new setting from the past, they closed their eyes, letting the emotions wash over them. Love, camaraderie, but above all, that unfathomable connection that transcends the limits of reality, permeated their every breath, perpetuating the miracle of their meeting.

Yes, history had sculpted them into soul mates, illuminating the horizon of their shared future with an eternal light. And as visitors wandered through the museum's corridors, captivated by the magic of the resurrected Opera House, Gabriel and Camille remained there, their eyes lost in infinity, aware that from now on, their own story would be forever intertwined with that of the pioneers who had paved the way before them. In this temple of knowledge frozen in the marble of centuries, the indelible imprint of their timeless bond would endure, defying the torments of time, to dazzle future generations, whispering the mysteries of an adventure that had brought together two beings destined to write the final lines of an exceptional chapter together.

Melodic sounds rose above the vaults of the Opera House, enveloping the audience in a spellbinding atmosphere. As the soft music rang out, Gabriel and Camille found themselves immersed in their memories, lost in the twists and turns of time. The crystalline notes seemed to carry echoes of the past, as if each touch of the piano or each vibration of the strings told an ancestral story. The faces of the members of the 19th-century clandestine circle formed in Gabriel's mind, and he could almost feel their presence among the audience.

Camille, meanwhile, felt the weight of the musical legacy of Aurélien, Gabriel's ancestor. She remembered the efforts made to decipher the scores, to unravel the mysteries buried in the harmonies and silences. Each measure was a fragile link between the present and the past, giving deep resonance to those events that had once been hidden. As he let himself be carried away by the enchanting music, Gabriel recalled the moments when he had discovered the first pieces of the puzzle, when his exploration of the Opera's hidden depths had led him on a mind-boggling quest. The secret room, the diaries, the play of light on engraved symbols: all of this took on a new depth, a renewed meaning in light of recent revelations. But beyond personal memories, it was the echoes of a troubled era that could be heard. The plots hatched by the Comte de Beaumont and his allies seemed to resonate across the decades, reminding us that history, far from being fixed, continued to cast its disturbing shadow over the present.

As the last note of Aurélien's symphony rang out, the faces of all those who had worked for the truth seemed to float in the room. Applause filled the space, but for Gabriel and Camille, it was as if a solemn silence enveloped this culmination. In that suspended moment, the echoes of history seemed to whisper that the lessons of the past remained immutable, ready to illuminate the path to a more enlightened future.

The yellowed pages of Aurélien's diary seemed to contain the timeless echoes of a bygone era. Gabriel contemplated the frail lines as if they held the mysteries of history within them. The last words were lost in a whirlwind of emotions, a subtle mixture of pain and hope. Each word was imbued with the grandeur of past struggles and the tragedy of intertwined destinies. As he began to read the final page, a strange peace permeated the atmosphere, as if time had been suspended to allow this story to finally find its harmony. The delicate characters seemed to still vibrate with the emotions that had once animated them. Aurélien had expressed his hopes, his doubts, but above all his unshakeable faith in justice and truth. Each word seemed enveloped in an aura of resilience and nobility, testifying to the inner strength of this ancestor with invisible scars. Across the centuries, this precious legacy resonated with a poignant urgency, like an elegiac message echoing through time.

The last notes of Aurélien's music still echoed

in the Opera House, filling the majestic space with poignant emotion. The previous notes seemed to float in the air, vibrant and charged with timeless stories. Gabriel and Camille stood side by side, overwhelmed by the power of the moment, by the deep connection that now bound them to these intertwined destinies.

As the audience applauded Aurélien's work, a solemn silence fell over the hall, as if everyone were holding their breath in tribute to the truth that had finally been revealed. The faces reflected a mixture of astonishment and gratitude, for the secrets of the past had now been unveiled, bringing light and redemption. Tears flowed among the audience, testifying to the profound impact of this masterful conclusion.

On stage, Gabriel took Camille's hand in a gesture of silent gratitude. Their eyes met, conveying a shared understanding, a harmony rediscovered in the face of adversity. They knew that their journey together had been much more than a simple investigation; it had been an intimate exploration of family ties, heritage, and resilience in the face of injustice.

As they left the Opera House, the crowd slowly dispersed, soaking up the lingering echoes of this unforgettable day. Gabriel felt his soul filled with a deep peace. At the same time, Camille clutched Aurélien's diary, containing the words of a restored past, close to her chest. They knew that this adventure would never leave them. Still, now it would be enveloped in a renewed serenity, a resurrected integrity. The last rays of the sun caressed the façades of the Opera House, bathing the building in a golden aura, symbolising a new chapter opening for this emblem of art and culture.

The history long buried beneath its foundations was now celebrated, honoured in all its splendour. A gentle smile appeared on Gabriel's lips, embodying silent gratitude to the heroes of the past, those courageous beings whose destiny had been erased. And so their odyssey came to an end, not in a grand tumult, but in the permanence of music transcending time, in the silent grandeur of truths finally revealed. The tunnel, where so many secrets had found refuge, would now remain open, a permanent witness to these intertwined destinies. Gabriel squeezed Camille's hand, signifying with this gesture all the gratitude and shared wonder for this extraordinary adventure. A page was turning, taking with it the echoes of a story written in the recesses of the Opera House, but graciously revealed to the world.

Twilight slowly envelops the chiselled reefs of the Opera House, as crowds fill every corner of the grand foyer. The guests, dressed in their finest attire, reflect in their eyes the promise of a rebirth. Beneath the majestic vaulted ceiling, the enchanting whispers of the ancient walls seem to awaken, finally recognising their rediscovered destiny. The smoke from incense mingles with the glow of candlelight, illuminating the gilding weathered by time.

The Opera House is decked out for its resurrection. At the centre of this elegant bustle, Gabriel and Camille walk forward with confident steps, united by the trials that have sealed their fate. Their knowing glances meet with an intensity marked by gratitude for this precious legacy that has been revealed. The murmurs of music from the past drift by in imperceptible echoes. They are the enlightened guardians of a revived memory, the silent actors of an unearthed story. Suddenly, the silence turns into a symphony of recognition. A solemn speech pours from the moved lips of an inspired storyteller, highlighting the driving forces that guided this quest for lost authenticity. Applause then bursts forth like a tribute, filling the space with warm recognition.

Guided by an infallible instinct, Gabriel and Camille recount their adventures, revealing the fabric woven between their intrepid hearts. Their voices harmonise, each becoming a faithful reflection of the emotions that fueled their quest. The enchanting amphitheatre absorbs their confidences, like a history offering, echoing the ancestral whispers of the Opera. Then, in an authentic gesture, the last page of Aurélien's diary is tenderly revealed. The words fly away, vibrating with tender melancholy, carrying truths long buried. The audience holds its breath, captivated by the spiritual testament of a man once forgotten, now revealed. Each syllable resonates, marking the end of an epic, but giving birth to an infinite series of timeless echoes.

The final note, Aurélien's, unfolds in a musical apotheosis, filling the space with its eternal lyricism. It connects the souls present to the imperishable legacy, weaving a bridge between the past and the present, offering the Opera a long-awaited redemption. In this suspended moment, old and new protagonists merge, celebrating the eternal ballet of time regained. And so our odyssey comes to an end, but in the memory of centuries forever sketched.